Vampire Kisses 2

Kissing Coffins

Ellen Schreiber

Vampire Kisses 2

Kissing Coffins

Katherine Tegen Books

An Imprint of HarperCollins*Publishers*

Vampire Kisses 2: Kissing Coffins

Copyright © 2005 by Ellen Schreiber

www.harperchildrens.com

Library of Congress Cataloging-in-Publication Data

Schreiber, Ellen.

Vampire kisses 2 : kissing coffins / Ellen Schreiber.— 1st ed.

p.   cm.

Sequel to: Vampire kisses

Summary: Sixteen-year-old Raven, a vampire-obsessed goth girl, searches for her true love, Alexander, who she has learned is a real vampire.

ISBN 0-06-077622-6 — ISBN 0-06-077623-4 (lib. bdg.)

[1. Vampires—Fiction.] I. Title: Vampire kisses two. II. Title: Kissing coffins. III. Title.

PZ7.S3787Vamb 2005   2005002510

[Fic]—dc22   CIP

                                                                                      AC

Typography by Sasha Illingworth

11 12 13 CG/RRDB 20 19 18 17 16 15

First Edition

To my father, Gary Schreiber,
with all my love,
from your little ghoul

CONTENTS

"Here's to new blood."

—Jagger Maxwell

I t was like a final nail in a coffin.

Becky and I were camped out in my darkened bedroom, engrossed in the eighties cult horror classic *Kissing Coffins*. The femme fatale, Jenny, a teenage, malnourished blond wearing a size negative-two white cotton dress, was desperately running up a serpentine rock footpath toward an isolated haunted mansion. Bright veins of lightning shot overhead in the pouring rain.

Only the night before had Jenny unearthed the true identity of her fiancé when she stumbled upon his hidden dungeon and found him climbing out of a coffin. The dashing Vladimir Livingston, a renowned English professor, was not a mere mortal after all, but an immortal blood-sucking vampire. Upon hearing Jenny's blood-curdling screams, Professor Livingston immediately covered his fangs with his black cape. His red eyes remained unconcealed, gazing back at her longingly.

"You cannot bear witness to me in this state," I said along with the vampire.

Jenny didn't flee. Instead, she reached out toward her fiancé. Her vampire love growled, reluctantly stepped back into the shadows, and disappeared.

The fang flick had gathered a goth cult following that continued today. Audience members flocked to retro cinemas in full costume, shouted the lines of the movie in unison, and acted out the various roles in front of the screen. Although I'd seen the movie a dozen times at home on DVD and knew all the words, I'd never been blessed with participating in a theatrical showing. This was Becky's first time watching it. We sat in my room, glued to the screen, as Jenny decided to return to the professor's mansion to confront her immortal lover. Becky dug her gnawed-on blood-red-painted fingernails into my arm as Jenny slowly opened the creaky wooden arch-shaped dungeon door. The ingénue softly crept down the massive winding staircase into Vladimir's darkened basement, torches and cobwebs hanging on the cement brick walls. A simple black coffin sat in the center of the room, earth sprinkled beneath it. She approached it cautiously. With all her might, Jenny lifted the heavy coffin lid.

Violins screeched to a climax. Jenny peered inside. The coffin was empty.

Becky gasped. "He's gone!"

Tears began to well in my eyes. It was like watching myself on-screen. My own love, Alexander Sterling, had vanished into the night two evenings ago, shortly after I had discovered he, too, was a vampire.

Jenny leaned over the empty casket and melodramatically wept as only a B-movie actress could.

A tear threatened to fall from my eye. I wiped it off with the back of my hand before Becky could see. I pressed the "Stop" button on the remote and the screen went black.

"Why did you turn it off?" Becky asked. Her disgruntled face was barely illuminated by the few votives I had scattered around my room. A tear rolling down her cheek caught the reflection of one of the candles. "It was just getting to the good part."

"I've seen this a hundred times," I said, rising, and ejected the DVD.

"But *I* haven't," she whined. "What happens next?"

"We can finish it next time," I reassured her as I put the DVD away in my closet.

"If Matt were a vampire," Becky pondered, referring to her khaki-clad new boyfriend, "I'd let him take a bite out of me anytime."

I felt challenged by her innocent remark, but I bit my tongue. I couldn't share my most secretest of secrets even with my best friend.

"Really, you don't know what you'd do" was all I could say.

"I'd let him bite me," she replied matter-of-factly.

"It's getting late," I said, turning on the light.

I hadn't slept the last two nights since Alexander left.

My eyes were blacker than the eye shadow I put on them.

"Yeah, I have to call Matt before nine," she said, glancing at my *Nightmare Before Christmas* alarm clock. "Would you and Alexander meet us for a movie tomorrow?" she asked, grabbing her jean jacket from the back of my computer chair.

"Uh . . . we can't," I stalled, blowing out the votives. "Maybe next week."

"Next week? But I haven't even seen him since the party."

"I told you, Alexander's studying for exams."

"Well, I'm sure he'll ace them," she said. "He's been cracking the books all day and night."

Of course, I couldn't tell anyone, even Becky, why Alexander had disappeared. I wasn't even sure of the reason myself.

But mostly, I couldn't admit to myself that he had gone. I was in denial. *Gone*—the word turned my stomach and choked my throat. Just the thought of explaining to my parents that Alexander had left Dullsville brought tears to my eyes. I couldn't bear accepting the truth, much less telling it.

And I didn't want another rumor mill circulating throughout Dullsville. If word got out that Alexander had moved without warning, who knows what conclusions the gossipmongers would jump to.

At this point, I wanted to maintain the status quo: keep up appearances until the RBI—Raven Bureau of Investigation—had a few more days to figure out a plan.

"We'll double-date soon," I promised as I walked Becky outside to her truck.

"I'm dying to know. . . ," she said, climbing into her pickup truck. "What happens to Jenny?"

"Uh . . . She tries to find Vladimir."

Becky closed her door, rolled down the window. "If I discovered Matt was a vampire and then he disappeared, I'd search for him," she said confidently. "I know you'd do the same for Alexander."

She started the engine and backed out of the driveway.

My best friend's remark was like a package of Pop Rocks blasting off in my brain. Why hadn't I thought of it sooner? I'd spent the last several days worrying how long I'd have to keep making excuses for Alexander's absence. Now I wouldn't be forced to wait an eternity in Dullsville wondering if he'd ever return. I didn't have to jump every time the telephone rang to find out it was for my mother.

I waved to Becky as she drove down the street. "You're right," I said to myself. "I have to find him!"

"I'm going to Alexander's. I won't be long—" I called to my mother as she sat devouring a J. Jill catalogue in the living room. I had a jolt of electricity coursing through my veins, which had been stagnant since my goth guy departed.

I grabbed my coat and ran back to the Mansion to find any clues of Alexander's whereabouts. I couldn't let my true love disappear without a full report from the RBI— Nancy Drew dipped in black.

Although becoming a vampire had always been a dream of mine, when faced with it, I didn't know what I'd do. Alexander already did what all great vampires do—he transformed me. I craved his presence every minute I was awake. I thirsted for his smile and hungered for his touch. So did I need to literally transform into a diva of darkness to be with my vampire boyfriend? Did I want to spend my life in greater isolation than I already did as an outcast goth? However, I had to let him know that I loved him no matter who or what he was.

I had spent a lifetime as a nocturnal-loving, rebellious, black-on-black-wearing outcast in the pearly white cliquey conservative town of Dullsville. I was relentlessly teased and bullied by soccer snob Trevor Mitchell. I was stared at like a circus freak by Dullsvillians, classmates, and teachers. The only friend I'd ever had was Becky, but we never shared the same taste in music or fashion, and our personalities were polar opposites. When Alexander Sterling moved to the Mansion on Benson Hill, for the first time in my life I felt like I wasn't alone. I was drawn to him before I even met him—seeing him standing in the darkened roadway, Becky's headlights illuminating his fair skin and sexy features. He took my breath away. Then, when he caught me sneaking into the Mansion and I got a glimpse of him again, I had a feeling I'd never known before. I knew I had to be with him.

Not only was he a pale-skinned, combat-boot-wearing goth like me, but as we began dating, I found out we listened to the same music—the Cure, Good Charlotte,

Evanescence. More important than tastes, we shared the same desires and dreams. Alexander understood loneliness, isolation, and being different. He knew firsthand what it was like to be judged for what he wore, how he looked, for being homeschooled and expressing himself through a paintbrush instead of a soccer ball.

When I was with him, I felt like I finally belonged. I wasn't judged, bullied, or teased for what I wore but was accepted, and even celebrated, for who I was inside.

With Alexander gone and his whereabouts unknown, I felt lonelier than I had before I met him.

I removed the brick that held the broken window open and crept inside the Mansion's basement. The full moon illuminated mirrors covered with white rumpled sheets, carelessly stacked cardboard boxes, and a coffin-shaped coffee table. My heart sank when I saw again that the earth-filled crates were gone.

The last time I had searched the Mansion uninvited, I had hoped to make chilling discoveries. I unearthed crates stamped by Romanian customs and marked SOIL. I found an ancient family tree, including Alexander's name, with no dates of births—or deaths. Now I was apprehensive about what I *wouldn't* find.

Upstairs, the portraits that once lined the walls were gone. I followed the hallway to the kitchen, where I opened the refrigerator. Only leftovers remained. Antique china dishes and pewter goblets still lined the cabinets. I spotted an unlit candle and a box of matches on the black granite countertop.

I wandered the empty halls by candlelight. The wooden floorboards creaked beneath my feet as if the lonely Mansion were crying.

In the living room the moonlight shone through the cracks in the red velvet drapes. The furniture was once again covered with white sheets. Disheartened, I headed for the grand staircase.

Instead of the music of the Smiths pulsing from upstairs, all I heard was the wind blowing against the shutters.

The ghoulish Mansion no longer sent waves of excitement through my veins, only lonely chills. I ascended the stairs and crept into the study, where I'd once been greeted by my knight of the night, holding fresh-picked daisies. Now it was just another abandoned library—books collecting dust, empty of readers.

The butler's bedroom was even more spartan, with a single perfectly made bed, Jameson's closet cleared of clothes, cloaks, and shoes.

The master bedroom was furnished with a canopy bed with black lace that dripped around its gothic columns. I stared at the mirrorless vanity directly across. The little combs, brushes, and nail polishes in shades of black, gray, and brown that had belonged to his mother were gone.

I'd never even had the opportunity to meet Alexander's parents. I wasn't sure if they even existed.

Tormented, I paused at the bottom of the attic steps. I wondered how Alexander felt leaving so suddenly, after finally being accepted by so many Dullsvillians.

I climbed the narrow attic stairway and blew out the

dripping candle. I entered his abandoned bedroom, which only two nights ago he had invited me into. His twin-sized mattress rested on the floor, unmade. Typical for any teenager, vampire or not.

The easel in the corner was bare. I gazed at the paint splattered on the floor. All his artwork was gone, even the painting he had made for me—a portrait of me dressed for the Snow Ball, holding a pumpkin basket and a Snickers, sporting a spider ring and fake vampire teeth.

A black letter-sized envelope lay on top of a blood-red paint can, sitting underneath the easel. I held the piece of mail up to the moonlight. It was addressed to Alexander and had a Romanian stamp. There was no return address and the postmark was illegible. The envelope had been ripped open.

Curiosity getting the best of me, I reached my fingers inside and pulled out a red letter. In black ink it read:

Alexander,
HE IS ON HIS WAY!

Unfortunately the rest of the letter had been torn off. I didn't know who it was from or what it meant. I wondered what vital information it held—maybe a top secret location. It was like watching a movie and not seeing the ending. And who was *he*?

I walked to the window and stared up at the moon—the very window where his grandmother's ghost was rumored to have been seen. I felt a kinship with the baroness. She had lost the love of her life and was left to keep his secret in isolation. I wondered if that would be my fate as well.

Where was Alexander headed? Back to Romania? I'd buy a ticket to Europe if I had to. I'd walk mansion door to mansion door to find him.

I wondered, if Alexander had stayed, what would have happened to him. If the town found out his identity, he could have been persecuted, taken away for scientific research, or paraded around as the top act in a sideshow. I imagined what would become of me. I might be interrogated by the FBI, hounded by tabloids, or forced to live in isolation, forever known as the Vampire Vulture.

I turned to leave his room when I saw a small booklet poking out from underneath his mattress. I took it to the attic window for closer inspection.

Had Alexander forgotten his passport? There was an empty spot where his photo had been torn out. I touched the space, wondering what picture a vampire could have taken.

I flipped through the pages. Stamps from England, Ireland, Italy, France, and the United States.

If I had Alexander's passport in my hand, he couldn't have gone back to Romania. No one can travel out of the country without a passport.

Now I had one thing I didn't have before.

Hope.

"Slow down!" my mom said when I burst through the kitchen door. "You're tracking mud all over the floor."

"I'll clean it later—" I said hurriedly.

"I'd like to invite Alexander over for dinner this week," she offered, catching up to me. "We haven't seen him since the party. You've been keeping him all to yourself."

"Sure—" I mumbled. "We'll talk later. I'm going to study."

"Study? You've been studying since the party. Alexander has had a positive effect on you," she said.

If my mother only knew I had been holed up in my room, waiting for e-mails, calls, and letters that never arrived.

Billy Boy and my dad were watching a basketball game in the den.

"When's Alexander coming over?" Billy asked when I passed by.

What could I tell him? Maybe never?

I quickly settled for, "Not for a while. I don't want to overexpose him to suburbia. He might want to start play-ing golf."

"I think you've found yourself a keeper," my dad complimented.

"Thanks, Dad," I said, stopping for a moment, think-ing of the family picnics, holidays, and vacations Alexander and I wouldn't be able to share. "Please don't disturb me," I ordered, heading toward my bat cave.

"Could she actually be doing homework?" Billy Boy asked my dad, surprised.

"I'm doing a report," I called back. "On vampires."

"I'm sure you'll get an A," my dad replied.

I locked myself in my bedroom and feverishly searched the Internet for any info on vampire hangouts where Alexander might be. New Orleans? New York? The six months sans sunlight of the North Pole? Would a vampire want to hide among the mortal population or isolate himself with his own kind?

Frustrated, I lay on my bed, boots still on, and stared at my bookshelves of Bram Stoker novels, movie posters of *The Lost Boys* and *Dracula 2000*, and my dresser top adorned with Hello Batty figures. But nothing gave me insight into where he might have gone.

I reached over to switch off my *Edward Scissorhands* lamp when I noticed on my nightstand the object that had gotten me into this mess: Ruby's compact!

Why hadn't I thought of her sooner? At the party, Jameson had asked her out for a date.

No one stands up Ruby—not even the undead!

The following morning I ran full throttle to Armstrong Travel, arriving before the agency opened.

I heard keys rattling and heels clicking behind me. It was Janice Armstrong, the owner.

"Where is Ruby?" I asked breathlessly.

"She doesn't come in on Tuesdays until the afternoon," she answered, opening the door.

"The afternoon?" I groaned.

"By the way," she said, moving close, "do you know anything about Alexander's butler?"

"Creepy Man?" I asked. "I mean, Jameson?"

"They were supposed to have a date," she confessed, switching on the office lights and adjusting the thermostat.

"How was it?" I asked naively.

Janice put her purse in her top drawer, turned on her computer, and looked at me.

"Don't you already know? He didn't show," she said. "And with a stunner like Ruby he was lucky she even looked in his direction!"

"Did he say why he canceled?" I pressed.

"No. I thought Alexander would have told you," she said.

"Not directly."

She shook her head. "A good man is hard to find, you know. But you have Alexander."

I bit my black lip.

"Hey, aren't you late for school?" she inquired, looking up at the Armstrong Travel clock.

"I'm always late! Janice, can you give me Ruby's address?"

"Why don't you stop back at the end of the day?"

"It's just that she left her compact—"

"You can leave it here," Janice suggested.

The front door opened and in walked Ruby.

I imagined a jaded woman in jeans holding a cigarette and a beer, but even being jilted, Ruby was in style. She was wearing full makeup and a white sweater and matching tight white slacks.

"You're in early today," Janice said.

"I have a lot to catch up on," Ruby replied with a sigh. "What are you doing here?" she asked, surprised to see me.

"I have something of yours."

"If you are here on behalf of Jameson," she said, "you can tell him I'm sorry *I* had to cancel."

"You? But he was—" I began.

Ruby settled in at her desk and turned on her computer, accidentally knocking over her cup of pens.

"Darn it!" she exclaimed, agitated, trying to grab the pens as they fell to the floor.

Janice and I raced over to help her pick them up.

"This has never happened before!" Ruby said angrily. "Now everyone will know."

"I knock things over all the time," I comforted.

"No, she means about Jameson," Janice whispered to me. "I got stood up several times before I met my Joe. But I must admit I'm surprised about the butler. It was doubly rude, since we came to the party to support the Sterling family." Janice glared at me as if Jameson's no-show was my fault. "I feel as though he stood me up, too."

"It's not the biggest deal," Ruby said. "Anyway, he's more . . . shall I say, eccentric than I am."

"He's a fool," Janice said.

"This really surprises me. He was such a gentleman," Ruby lamented. "And that accent. I guess that's why I was taken by him."

"He likes you, too," I said. "Only—"

Both women looked at me as if I were going to reveal national secrets.

"Only what?" Janice asked.

"Only . . . that he should have called."

"You're darn right! I hope you haven't told anyone about this," Ruby said worriedly. "In a small town like this, being stood up could ruin my reputation."

"You must know something, Raven," Janice pried.

"Yes, did Alexander allude to anything?" Ruby asked.

I had to console my former boss. After all, I was the one who caused Jameson to abandon their date. I couldn't let Ruby take it personally.

"Just that the reason he canceled had nothing to do with you," I said evasively.

"I bet he has a girlfriend," Ruby speculated. "I read in *Cosmo*—"

"Of course he doesn't!" I exclaimed with a laugh. "But I need to know something as well. Did Jameson have a trip planned?"

"Do you know something I don't?"

"Did he buy any airline tickets? Or come in asking for any road maps?" I hinted.

"What aren't you telling us?"

Ruby and Janice stared at me hard. I wasn't about to tell them the truth—that Alexander didn't reflect in her compact.

Ruby's compact! I almost forgot.

I began to pull it out from my purse when a man dressed in chinos and a red polo shirt entered the office with a grand bouquet. Distracted, I replaced the compact and zipped up my purse.

"Ruby White?" he asked.

"I'm Ruby," she said, her hand waving in the air like she'd just won the coverall at bingo.

He handed Ruby a bouquet of white roses. She blushed as she took the flowers.

Flowers for Ruby? They could have been sent from any number of Dullsvillian suitors.

"What does the card say?" Janice asked eagerly. "I wonder if they're from Kyle the golf pro."

"'I'm sorry these had to greet you instead of me,'" Ruby read. She looked up in astonishment. "'Fondly, Jameson.'"

"Jameson?" I asked, suddenly wide-eyed.

"How sweet!" Janice said, filling a glass vase from the watercooler. "I told you all along he was wonderful."

"Can you believe this?" Ruby wondered aloud, holding the bouquet close.

"What else does it say?" I asked.

"Isn't that enough?" Janice said, inhaling the scent and placing the flowers in the vase. "They're beautiful!"

"No info on where the order was placed from?" I inquired.

Ruby shook her head, distracted.

"But there has to be—" I mumbled. I looked out the window and saw the deliveryman stepping into a white van with the words FLOWER POWER spelled out in daisies.

I raced out the door as the van began to drive off.

"Wait!" I called, running hard in my combat boots. "You forgot something!"

But it was too late. The van sped around the corner.

Breathless and frustrated, I retreated back to the travel agency. I began to open the door when I noticed a piece of paper lying on the sidewalk. It was a Flower Power delivery order. It must have fallen out of the van. I quickly grabbed it, scanning the document for any vital info. The travel agency address was fully disclosed. But the sender's address was blank. No name. No e-mail. Nothing.

Then, hidden in the right-hand corner, I noticed a ten-digit number.

"Can I use your phone, Ruby?" I asked, running inside. "I'll only be a minute."

"Of course," she said, arranging the roses. At that moment, I could have called Africa and she wouldn't have cared.

The area code seemed oddly familiar. I racked my brain. It belonged to a town a couple hundred miles away, where my aunt Libby lived.

I dialed. Would Alexander's voice greet me? *Ring.* Or Creepy Man's? *Ring.* Or would it be a dead end? *Ring.*

"Thank you for calling the Coffin Club," a zombie-like voice finally answered. "Our business hours are nightly from sunset to sunrise. Leave a message—if you dare!"

I let the phone slip from my hand. Ruby was still arranging her flowers.

"Good goth!" I whispered. "The Coffin Club!"

At school I now experienced a newfound popularity. It wasn't as if I were a celebrity, but schoolmates who had never even looked my way before called, "What's up, Raven?"

But besides a hello wave, nothing had changed. No one except Matt and Becky invited me to eat lunch, offered me a ride home, or asked me to join their study group. Not one classmate secretly passed me a note or bothered to share his pack of gum. Thankfully, I was too distracted to appreciate any rise in status and spent a morbidly long afternoon in front of the library computer searching the Internet for the Coffin Club.

"I want to visit Aunt Libby," I told my parents that night at dinner.

"Aunt Libby?" my dad asked. "We haven't seen her in ages."

"I know. And it's about time. Spring break starts Wednesday. I'd like to leave tomorrow afternoon."

"I can't imagine you'd want to be away from Alexander for a minute, much less a few days," my mom said.

"Of course I'll die being away from Alexander," I exclaimed, rolling my eyes. I could feel my family staring at me, waiting for my next response. "But he's going to be tied up with his homeschooling exams. So I thought I'd take the opportunity to see Aunt Libby."

My parents looked at each other.

"Are you sure you're not going there to see a Wicked Wiccas concert?"

"Dad! They broke up five years ago."

"Well, Libby's not a very good role model," my dad remarked. "And who knows what neurotic guy she's involved with this time."

"Dad, she's more like you than you think. You just don't drive a hippie mobile anymore."

"I remember visiting *my* aunt when I was a teenager," my mom said. "She took me to see *Hair.*"

"See—I need these memorable teen experiences to shape my life."

"Libby gets such a kick out of Raven," she admitted. "It would be good for her as well."

"All right," Dad said reluctantly. "I'll call her tonight. But if she's still practicing voodoo, you're not going."

After dinner I met Becky by the swings at Evans Park.

"I had to talk to you, pronto," I began.

"Me, too! Life is so good. Can you believe we both have boyfriends?"

Even if Alexander weren't a vampire, the idea of us having boyfriends was still unreal. We'd both been social outcasts for so many years, it was incomprehensible to be accepted by anyone but each other.

"I need you to come on a little trip with me," I told her.

"Trip?"

"I'm going to visit my aunt Libby and I need you to come!" I exclaimed excitedly.

"This weekend? I'll have to ask."

"No, I'm leaving tomorrow afternoon."

"Matt asked me to watch his soccer game after school."

"You just started seeing him!" I argued.

"I thought you'd be happy for me. Besides, I was going to ask you to come."

The thought of watching a soccer game made me want to hurl, but Becky's glow made me realize I was being selfish. "I *am* happy for you, but—"

"Can't you go another time?" she begged. "We have all spring break to hang out with Matt and Alexander."

There was no point arguing. Becky was going to watch Matt's game tomorrow, just as I was going to search for Alexander. No amount of pleading would make us change our minds. Now that Matt had abandoned his best friend, my nemesis, Trevor, the thorn in my side since kindergarten, he would hang out with Becky all the time. And I was jealous of Becky for having a boyfriend who hadn't disappeared into the night.

"Why is this trip so important?" she asked.

"It's top secret."

"What's top secret?" Matt inquired, appearing behind us.

"What are you doing here?" I asked, startled. "This is a private meeting."

"Becky and I are going to Ace's Arcade. She told me to meet her here."

It was bad enough I was losing Alexander to the Underworld, but when I needed my best friend the most, I was losing her to 3-D pinball.

"I gotta go," I said, turning away.

"So what was your top secret news?" Matt asked. "It'll be great to hear something other than Trevor's bogus stories for once."

I stared at the happy couple—Cupid's newest bull's-eyes.

"Trevor was right. The Sterlings really *are* vampires," I said impulsively.

They stared at me like I was crazy. Then they burst into laughter.

I, too, laughed and then walked away.

I packed my suitcase full of black garments, unsure of what I was preparing for. To be safe I also packed a clove of garlic in Tupperware, Ruby's compact, and a can of Mace.

To calm my nerves, I opened my Olivia Outcast journal and made a list of Positives of Dating a Vampire:

1. He'll be around for eternity.
2. He can always fly for free.
3. I'll save hundreds of dollars on wedding photos.
4. No mirrors to Windex.
5. He'll never have garlic breath.

I closed my journal. I had one more thing to pack.

I opened the door to my brother's room. Billy was tapping his skinny fingers on his computer keyboard.

"What do you want?" he snapped when I peeked in.

"Want? It's not what I want, but rather what I have to give. I picked this up after school today from Software City. They said it was the latest."

I showed him *Wrestling Maniacs 3*.

"Did you steal it?"

"Of course not—I may be weird, but I'm not a thief!"

He reached for the game, but I held it firm. "I just need one thing in return."

He rolled his eyes. "I knew it!"

"It's just teensy-weensy."

"Answers to a test?" he guessed.

"Not this time."

"Need a paper written?"

"Not yet."

"Then what?"

"I need a fake ID," I whispered.

"Aunt Libby is not going to take you to a bar!"

"Of course she's not. But it's really for identification, since I won't have my driver's license for a few months."

"Use your school ID, then."

"I need to be eighteen!" I started to shout. Then I took a deep breath. "There's a library convention, and I need to be eighteen to check out books."

"Whatever! Mom and Dad will kill you! You're too young to drink."

"I'm not going to drink. I just want to hang out."

"What would Alexander say if he found that you were going cruising without him?"

"I'm hoping to meet him there," I whispered.

"I knew it! You couldn't care less about 'my favorite aunt Libby,'" he said in a girlie voice.

"Pretty please?" I asked, dangling the game before his computer-strained eyes.

"Well . . ."

"You'll make it?"

"No, but I know someone who will."

For the first time ever I walked my brother to school—Dullsville Middle. The redbrick building, front lawn, and playground looked surprisingly smaller than when I had attended several years ago.

"I used to skip class and hide out over there," I said, pointing to a small athletics equipment shed.

"I know," he said. "'Raven was here' is scratched all over the side."

"I guess I skipped more than I thought," I said with a grin.

I felt like a towering gothic giant as I walked up the

front lawn among girls sporting Bratz T-shirts and Strawberry Shortcake notebooks and boys with overstuffed Pokemon backpacks.

I figured we were meeting a corrupt shop teacher, but instead we were greeted at the entrance by an eleven-year-old red-haired wunderkind named Henry.

"What do you need to make fake IDs for?" I asked him. "Getting into Chuck E. Cheese's after hours?"

Billy Boy's friend gazed up at me, like he'd never seen a real girl up close.

"You can stare at my picture *after* you take it," I joked.

"Follow me," he said.

In the hallway we were stopped by Mrs. Hanley, my sixth grade math teacher.

"Raven Madison! You look so grown up!"

I could tell she had expected me to wind up in juvie hall or shipped off to a boarding school. She stared at my brother and me, obviously wondering how two such different human beings could come from the same shared DNA.

"I never realized Billy was your brother," she confessed.

"I know," I whispered. "I'm amazed, too."

"Well, some things haven't changed," she said, walking off. She kept looking back as if she had seen an apparition. I knew who'd be the subject of today's talk around the microwave in the teachers' lounge.

We stopped at Henry's locker, the only one with a combination lock that was hooked up to a garage door opener. Henry flipped the control switch and the combo lock sprung open. Computer games, electronics, and programming manuals were organized in racks like a miniature computer store.

He pulled out a digital camera hidden underneath a shelf.

"Let's go."

I followed them around the corner to the computer room. But it was locked. My heart sank.

"This can't happen! Break a window if you have to," I said, half jokingly.

Both geeky preteens looked at me as if I were the odd one.

Henry dug into the back pocket of his chinos and pulled out a worn brown leather wallet. He opened it and got out a credit card. He slid the card into the door, jiggled it a little, and within a moment the door slipped open.

"I like your style," I said with a smile.

Twenty minutes later I was staring at an eighteen-year-old Raven. "I look good for my age," I said with a wink, and headed for home.

"Mom, I'm not going to Siberia. I'll be back in two days." We were sitting at Dullsville's Greyhound bus stop, outside Shirley's Ice Cream Parlor. She was trying to strangle me with kisses when the bus squealed to the curb in front of a few other young Dullsvillians heading out early for spring break.

As the bus pulled away and I waved good-bye from my window seat in the back, I actually felt a pang in my stomach. This would be my first trip away from Dullsville on my own. I even wondered if I would return.

I sat back, closed my eyes, and thought what it would be like if I became Alexander's vampiress.

I imagined Alexander waiting for me at Hipsterville's bus stop, standing in the rain, wearing tight black jeans and a glow-in-the-dark Jack Skellington shirt, a small bouquet of black roses in one hand. Upon seeing me, his pale face would flush with just enough pink to make him look alive. He'd take my hand in his, lean into me, and kiss me long. He would whisk me off in his restored vintage hearse, adorned with painted spiders and cobwebs, the music of Slipknot blasting from the speakers.

We'd park in front of an abandoned castle and climb the creaky spiral stairs that led to the desolate tower. The ancient castle walls would be lined with black lace and the rustic wooden floors sprinkled with rose petals. A million candles would flicker around the room, the skinny medieval windows barely letting in moonlight.

"I couldn't be without you anymore," Alexander would say. He would lean into me and take my neck into his mouth. I'd feel a slight pressure on my flesh. I'd become dizzy, but feel more alive than I'd ever felt before—my head would slump back, my body become limp in his arms. My heart would pulse in overtime as if beating for both of us. Out of the corner of my eye, I would be able to see Alexander lift his head proudly.

He'd gently let me down. I'd feel lightheaded and stumble to my feet, holding my red-stained neck as the blood trickled down my forearm.

I'd be able to feel two pointy fangs with the tip of my tongue.

He would open a tower window to reveal the sleeping town. I'd be able to see things I'd never seen before, like smiling ghosts floating above the houses.

Alexander would take my hand, and we would fly off into the night, above the sparkling lights of the town and beneath the twinkling stars, like two gothic fairies.

The sound of clanging bells interrupted. Not the tin-kling of bells signaling my arrival into the Underworld, but rather a railroad crossing warning of an incoming train, signaling the end of my overactive imagination. The bus was stopped in front of a railroad track. A toddler in the seat across the aisle from me waved excitedly as the black engine approached.

"Chug-a-chug-a-choo-choo!" he exclaimed. "I want to be a conductor," he proclaimed to his mother.

I, too, stared as the conductor waved his blue hat while the train began to pass us. Instead of new boxcars whizzing by us, a string of dilapidated, graffiti-laden freight cars lagged in front of us. Like the toddler across from me, who was likely dreaming of the glamorous life of a conductor—too naive to realize the demands of the job, isolation, long hours, and little pay—I, too, wondered if my dream of becoming a vampire was more romantic than its reality.

I was stepping into a world of the unknown, knowing only one thing: I had to find Alexander.

The official welcome sign to Aunt Libby's town should read, "Welcome to Hipsterville—Inhabitants must check all golf pants at the city limits." The small town was an eclectic mix of hip coffee shops, upscale secondhand stores, and indie cinemas where all forms of cool people presided—granola heads, artists, goths, and chic freaks. Every kind was acceptable here. I could see why Alexander and Jameson might have escaped to this particular town. It was in close proximity to Dullsville and they could easily blend in with the smorgasbord of other motley inhabitants.

I could only imagine what my life would have been like if I had grown up in a town where I was more accepted than ostracized. I could have been on the A-list to Friday night "haunted" house parties, been crowned Halloween Queen, and received straight A's in Historical Tombstones class.

Dad and Aunt Libby had both been hippies in the sixties, but while Dad morphed into a yuppie, Libby stayed true to her inner Deadhead. She had moved to Hipsterville, majored in theater at the university, and now worked as a waitress in a vegan restaurant to support her acting. She was always performing in an avant-garde play or a performance-art piece in some director's garage. When I was eleven my family watched her stand onstage for what seem liked days, dressed as a giant snow pea and speaking in broken sentences about how she sprouted.

When I arrived in Hipsterville, I wasn't shocked to find that Alexander wasn't waiting for me, but I was surprised my aunt wasn't. *I hope she isn't this late for her curtain calls,* I thought, as I waited at the bus stop in the hot sun beside my suitcase. Finally I spotted her beat-up vintage yellow Beetle sputtering into the lot.

"You're so grown up!" she exclaimed, getting out of her car and giving me a huge hug. "But you dress the same. I was counting on that."

Aunt Libby had a youthful face, decorated with sparkling purple eye shadow and pink lipstick. She wore red dangly crystal earrings beneath her auburn hair, a sky blue halter dress spotted with white beads, and beige Nairobi sandals.

Her warmth spilled over me. Even though we differed

in our tastes, we immediately bonded like sisters, talking about fashion, music, and movies.

"*Kissing Coffins?*" she asked when I told her what I recently watched. "That's like *The Rocky Horror Picture Show*. I remember going to the midnight show and dancing in the aisles. 'Let's do the time warp again,'" Aunt Libby sang, as passersby gave us strange looks.

"Uh, *Kissing Coffins* isn't a musical," I interrupted before my aunt got a citation for disturbing the peace.

"Isn't that a shame. Well, I've got a great place to take you," she raved, and led me around the block to Hot Gothics.

"Wow!" I shouted, pointing to a pair of black patent-leather boots and a torn black mesh sweater. "I've only seen this store on the Internet."

I was in goth heaven, and it was beautiful! Wicked Wiccas T-shirts, Hello Batty comics, and fake body tattoos.

The multipierced fuchsia-haired clerk in black shorts over black leggings, three-inch-heeled Mary Janes, and a gray mechanics shirt that said "Bob" walked over to me. She had the kind of style that in Dullsville could be seen only on satellite TV. And instead of my usual retail experience of either being ignored or seen as a potential thief, she greeted me as if I were a movie star at a Beverly Hills boutique.

"Can I help you? We have tons of stuff on sale."

I eagerly followed her around the store until I was exhausted from rack after rack of gothic clothing.

"Feel free to ask, if you need anything else," she said.

I had my arms stuffed with fishnet stockings, knee-high black boots, and an Olivia Outcast purse.

Libby modeled a black T-shirt that read "Vampires Suck."

I felt a pang in my heart and a lump in my throat.

"I'll buy it for you," she insisted, taking it to the cash register.

Normally I would have screamed with delight at a shirt like that. But now it only reminded me that Alexander was gone.

"You don't have to."

"Of course I do. I'm your aunt. We'll take this," she said, handing the clerk the shirt and her credit card.

I held my gothic goodies. Everything reminded me of Alexander.

"I'll just put these back," I said. But then I thought about how sexy I'd look in boots and black fishnets, if I found him again.

"We'll get these, too," my aunt said, seeing through me, and handed the clerk my merchandise.

Aunt Libby lived on a tiny tree-lined urban street with skinny row-house apartments from the 1940s—a sharp contrast to my contemporary suburban house and neighborhood in Dullsville. Her one-bedroom apartment was small but cozy, with a bohemian feel—flowered rugs, pillows, wicker chairs, and lavender potpourri filled the living room. Italian masks decorated the walls and Chinese lanterns hung from the ceiling.

"You can crash here," Aunt Libby said, pointing to a paisley futon couch in the living room.

"Thanks!" I said, excited about my new digs. "I appreciate you letting me visit you."

"I'm so happy you came!" she replied.

I placed my suitcase by the futon and glanced at a Pink Floyd clock hanging above the antique "just for show" fireplace, which she had filled with unlit candles. I had only a few hours until sunset.

Libby poured me carrot juice as I unpacked. "You must be hungry," she called from her tiny art deco kitchen. "You want an avocado wrap?"

"Sure," I said, plopping down at her vintage weathered-yellow dinner table with a beaded napkin holder and a wobbly leg. "I bet you have a hot date tonight," I hinted, as she topped my sandwich with sprouts. "But that's okay. I can take care of myself."

"Didn't your father tell you? I guess he wanted it to be a surprise."

"Tell me what?" I asked, envisioning Libby handing me VIP passes to the Coffin Club.

"I have a show tonight."

A show? I didn't travel all the way to Hipsterville to spend three hours sitting in a garage.

"It's downtown," she said proudly. "We're having a private performance tonight for the town's senior citizens, so I'm sorry to say you'll be the only one there without gray hair. But I know you'll love it." She grabbed an envelope hanging on her fridge by a rainbow magnet.

She opened the envelope, pulled out a ticket, and presented it to me.

THE VILLAGE PLAYERS PRESENT
Dracula

The Village Players performed in a former elementary school. The actresses' dressing room was a classroom that still smelled of erasers, and the large windows were covered with heavy shades. Mirrors replaced the chalkboard, and a long vanity lined with makeup cases, flowers, and congratulations cards sat in place of a teacher's desk.

As Aunt Libby applied her makeup and squirmed into her white Victorian dress, I spun a forgotten globe in the corner, letting a black-painted fingernail come to a rest on Romania.

Of course, under any other circumstances I would have loved to see a performance of *Dracula*. I would have gone every night, especially to see my aunt as an admittedly old, but I'm sure convincing, Lucy. I would have ordered front-row seats. But why would I want to see a fake Dracula when I could see the real thing sipping a Bloody Mary down the street at the Coffin Club?

The stage manager called from the hallway, "Five minutes."

I hugged Libby and told her to break a leg. I hoped she wouldn't notice my empty seat during the performance, but I couldn't worry about that as I hurried up the aisle to the back of the theater.

I pulled aside an elderly usher who looked like he might be one of the undead. "Which way to the Coffin Club?"

Some people spend all their lives searching for their soul mates. I had only an hour and a half to find mine.

I turned the corner to a sight I'd never seen before: More
than a dozen young goths waiting in a line. Spiked, dyed
black-and-white hair, purple floor-length extensions, bil-
lowy capes, knee-high black boots, and Morticia dresses.
Lips, cheeks, tongues, foreheads pierced with metal studs
and chains. Tattoos of bats, barbed wire, and esoteric
designs covered their limbs, chests, and backs and, in many
cases, their entire flesh.

Above the line of ghoulish goths, two coffins were
outlined in red neon on the black brick building.

Impatience being my virtue, I snuck in front of a girl
who was tying up loose corset laces in her medieval gown.

A Marilyn Manson look-alike standing in front of me
turned to face me. "You from around here?"

"I don't think any of us are from around here, if you
know what I mean," I said, all knowing.

"I'm Primus," he responded, extending his hand. His

fingernails were longer than mine.

"I'm Raven," I replied.

"And I'm Poison," a girl in a tight black-and-red-striped rayon dress snapped, grabbing Primus's hand away.

The crowd continued moving forward. Primus and Poison showed their IDs and disappeared inside.

A bouncer in a *Nosferatu* T-shirt scrutinized me, blocking the black, wooden coffin-shaped door.

I held my card proudly. But when the devilish-looking bouncer started studying it, my confidence waned and my heart began to pound.

"This looks like it was taken yesterday."

"Well, it wasn't," I said with a sneer. "It was taken today."

The bouncer cracked a smile, then laughed. "I haven't seen you here before."

"Don't you remember me from last time? I was the girl in black."

The bouncer laughed again. He stamped my hand with an image of a bat and wrapped a barbed-wire-shaped plastic bracelet around my left wrist. "Here alone?" he asked.

"I'm hoping to meet a friend. An older dude, bald with a gray cloak. He was here recently. Have you seen him?"

The bouncer shrugged. "I only remember the girls," he said with a smile. "But, if he doesn't show, I'm off just before sunrise," he added, letting me pass and opening the coffin door.

I stepped through and entered a dark, crowded, smoke-filled, head-banging Underworld. I had to pause to let my eyes adjust.

Dry-ice fog floated over the clubsters like tiny ghosts. The cement walls were spray-painted black, with flashing neon headstones. Pale mannequins with huge bat wings hung from the ceiling, some bound in leather, others in Victorian suits or antique dresses. The bathroom doors were shaped like giant tombstones; one read MONSTERS and the other GHOULS. Spiderwebs clung to the bottles behind the bar. A sign underneath a broken clock read NO GARLIC. Next to the dance floor a mini gothic flea market was set up on folding tables. A vampire clubster could buy anything from fake teeth to body tattoos and tarot card readings. A balcony loomed above the dance floor, accessible by a spiral staircase. Clubsters, with blood-filled amulets dangling from their necks and grimacing vampire teeth, seemed to be a mix of harmless outcast goths and maybe a few truly deranged. But if I had to bank that there were real vampires in this part of the world, some had to be mixing it up here, where they could walk hidden among the masses.

The thrashing music of Nightshade blasted from the speakers. I could feel the stares as I walked by. Instead of the usual glares I was used to enduring whether walking down the halls of Dullsville High or sauntering past Prada-bes milling about town, I felt self-conscious for a different reason—I was being checked out. Hot Goths, Gorgeous Goths, even Geeky Goths were eyeing me as if I were a gothic Paris Hilton catwalking down a medieval runway. Even girls, sporting shrunken T-shirts that read SIN or pretentiously exposed their concave, multipierced bellies, scrutinized me territorially, as if threatened by any other single female with black eye shadow in a tight black dress. I fingered my raven-colored hair nervously, trying to be careful whom I made eye contact with. Were they real vampires smelling the scent of a mortal? Or just goths looking for a ghoul?

I pushed my way to the bar, where a long-haired bartender wearing lipstick and eye shadow was pouring red liquor into a martini glass.

"What can I get for you?" he asked. "Blood beer or an Execution?"

"I'd like an Execution, but make it a virgin," I replied with confidence. "I'm driving. Or should I say *flying*."

The grim bartender broke into a smile. He took two pewter bottles off the shelf and poured them into an iron-maiden-shaped glass.

"That'll be nine dollars."

"Can I keep the glass?" I asked. I sounded like an excited kid at an amusement park instead of an underage teen trying to be cool at a bar.

I handed him a ten. "Keep the change," I said proudly, like I'd seen my dad do a thousand times. I wasn't even sure I was leaving a proper tip.

I took a sip of the red slush, which tasted like tomato juice.

"Was a bald man wearing a dark cloak here the other night?" I asked, shouting over the blaring music. "He made a phone call from the club."

"That guy's here every night."

I smiled eagerly. "Really?"

"And at least fifty guys just like him," he answered loudly.

I turned around. He was right. There were as many shaved heads as there were spiked ones.

"He has creepy-looking eyes and a Romanian accent," I added.

"Oh, that dude?" he asked, pointing to a skinny, bald man with a gray cloak, talking to a girl in a Wednesday Addams dress in the corner.

"Thanks!"

I quickly pushed my way through the crowd.

"Jameson!" I shouted, tapping him on the shoulder. "It's me!"

He turned around. But instead of actually being a senior citizen, he just looked like one. I fled before he could ask me to bond with him for eternity.

I scooted by the gothic marketplace, not having time to stop and purchase pewter, crystal, or silver amulets or have my tarot cards read.

But when I passed the last booth, a palm reader grabbed my hand. "You are looking for love," she said.

A single girl in a club looking for love? What were the odds of that?

"Well, where is he?" I challenged, shouting over the blaring music.

"He's closer than you think," she answered mysteriously.

I glanced around the packed club. "Where?" I hollered.

The reader said nothing.

I slipped a couple of dollars into her palm. "Which direction?" I asked loudly.

She looked into my eyes. "East."

"The bar?"

"You must look in here," she said, and pointed with her other hand to her heart.

"I don't need pithy sayings. I need a map!" I chided, and continued to make my way through the crowd.

I stopped at the DJ booth.

"Did you see a bald man here recently?" I asked the DJ, who was dressed in a white lab coat with fake blood splattered on it.

"Who?"

"Did you see a bald man here last weekend?" I repeated.

He shrugged his shoulders.

"He may have been wearing a gray cloak."

"Who?"

"The man I'm asking about!" The music was so loud, even I couldn't hear myself.

"Ask Romeo at the bar," he hollered back.

"I already did!" I grumbled.

As I returned to the bar, I spotted a dark-haired guy in jeans and a charcoal gray T-shirt leaning against a Corinthian column on the dance floor.

I pushed past the clubsters, my heart beating full force. "Alexander?"

But on closer inspection, I was confronted with a twenty-something wearing a BITE ME T-shirt and reeking of alcohol.

Frustrated, I headed back to the bar once again.

"That wasn't him," I said to Romeo. "The guy I'm talking about made a phone call from the Coffin Club."

Romeo turned to his Elviraish counterpart, who was placing a tip into her bra.

"Hey, this girl's looking for a bald guy who came to the club the other night," Romeo said. "He made a phone call from here."

"Oh, yeah, that sounds familiar," she said.

"Really?" I perked up.

"I remember because he asked to use the phone. No one asks anymore. Everyone has a cell."

"Did he tell you where he was staying?"

"No. He just said thank you and gave me a twenty for handing him our phone."

"Was he with anyone?" I asked, eager to receive news of Alexander.

"I think I saw him hanging out with a guy in a Dracula cape."

"Alexander?" I asked excitedly. "Was his name Alexander Sterling?"

Romeo looked at me as if he had recognized the name, but then turned away to wipe down the bar.

"I didn't have time for introductions," Elvira said. She turned away from me and waited on a guy dressed in leather waving a twenty.

Jameson *had* been here! And possibly Alexander, in the cape he had worn on the last night I saw him.

I looked around the club for any signs that might help me find him. Maybe Alexander found this place completely bogus. Was this club just full of outcast goths like me, or were any of them real vampires? Then I remembered the way to spot a true vampire was by *not* looking at them.

I reached into my purse and pulled out Ruby's compact. Every fanged clubster around me reflected back. I had to think of another plan. I replaced the compact and headed for the door.

Suddenly I felt a cold hand on my shoulder.

I turned around.

"I think I know who you want to see," Romeo said.

"You do?"

"Follow me."

I hung close to my gothic usher, half exhilarated, half terrified.

He led me up the spiral staircase to the balcony. A shadowy figure sat on a coffin-shaped couch, a large goblet and a candelabra before him on a round coffee table.

The mysterious figure glared up at me. I felt a sudden chill. I could barely whisper, "Alexander—"

The lone figure pulled the candelabra close, illuminating his features.

It wasn't Alexander.

Instead, sitting in front of me was a cryptic-looking teen, his cadaverous yet attractive face almost hidden beneath dripping white hair with red ends, as if they had been dipped in blood. Three silver rings pierced his eyebrow, and a pewter skeleton hung from his left ear. His seductive eyes pierced through me, one metallic green, the other ice blue. The whites were filled with spiderwebbed veins, as if he'd been awake for days. His skin was the color of death. His fingernails were painted black, like mine, and he wore a tattoo on his arm, which read POSSESS.

It took all my strength to turn away from his intoxicating gaze, as if I were trying to break an unearthly spell.

"You look disappointed," he said in a seductive voice, forcing me to gaze back at him. "You were expecting to meet someone else?"

"Yes. I mean . . . no."

"Hoping for someone to bond with for eternity? Someone who won't run away from you?"

"Aren't we all?" I snapped back.

"Well, I just may be your man."

"I think Romeo was confused," I said. "I was looking for someone who made a phone call from here. An older, bald man."

"Really? He doesn't seem your type."

"I was obviously mistaken—"

"One person's mistake is another man's destiny. I'm Jagger," he said with a piercing glare that made my blood boil. He stood and offered a pale hand.

"I'm Raven, but—"

"You are looking for someone who can help you fulfill your darkest desires."

"No, I was looking for . . . ," I began naively.

"Yes?" Jagger asked, with a cunning smile.

Something didn't feel right. Hadn't Romeo already told him who I was looking for? Intuition overcame me.

Jagger seemed too eager to hear me name someone.

"I've really got to go," I said, clutching my purse close like a shield.

"Please, join me." He grabbed my arm and pulled me onto the couch. "I believe we have a lot in common."

"Maybe next time . . . I really have to go—"

"Romeo, get the lady a drink," Jagger commanded. "How about a Death Sentence? It's the club special."

Jagger inched toward me and gently stroked my hair away from my shoulder.

"You're quite beautiful," he said.

I avoided his gaze and clutched my purse in my lap while he continued to eye me. I sensed that this seductive good-looking goth was no more my friend than Trevor.

"Listen, you have been—" I began, trying to stand up, when Romeo returned with two goblets.

"Here's to new blood," said Jagger with a laugh.

I hesitantly clinked my goblet with his. He took a long gulp, then waited for me to do the same. With a guy this nefarious, I could only imagine what the drink might have been laced with.

"I've gotta go," I said, standing up.

"He's not like you think he is," he said.

I paused, almost frozen. "I don't know who you are talking about," I replied, and turned to leave.

"We'll find him together," Jagger said, and rose from the couch to block my path.

He winked at me, and then grinned, revealing sharp vampire fangs that glistened in the candlelight. I stepped back, and then realized that in the Coffin Club everyone had fangs.

There was only one way to confirm who or what Jagger was.

"Okay. I'll give you my number," I said, turning away from him. I reached into my purse and sheltered the compact from his view. "Just let me find my pen."

My fingers shook as I opened Ruby's compact and angled it in his direction. I closed my eyes and hesitated. I took a deep breath and opened them.

But Jagger had already disappeared.

6

Dracula Delivers

I returned to the Village Players Theater just in time for curtain call. I hurried backstage, where I was greeted by a worried Lucy in the dressing room.

"I didn't see you in the audience!" Aunt Libby said in a tone that resembled my mother's.

"Aren't you supposed to be concentrating on the show?"

"How could I concentrate when all I saw was your empty seat?" she snapped.

"A woman next to me kept falling asleep on me," I fibbed, "so I moved to the back row. But you were wonderful!"

"So you did see it," she responded, relieved.

"Of course!" I gave her a big squeeze. "Wild vampires couldn't pull me away."

I fiddled through her makeup kit while she greeted a few fans in the hallway. I couldn't shake my encounter with Jagger from my head. Had I met a second Dracula? Or was Jagger just some tattooed teen thirsting for a date?

"You have to meet Marshall," Aunt Libby called when she returned to the dressing room.

I was peeking beneath the window shade at a lone figure lurking in the darkened alley by the Dumpster.

"Raven!" Aunt Libby called.

I turned around to face the Village Players version of Dracula—a malnourished, overpowdered, middle-aged man with slicked-back, gelatinized gray hair, ultra-red lips that resembled Bozo the Clown's, and oversized press-on fingernails. He wore a traditional satin cape.

How could an overaged, uncharismatic man play the sexy, seductive Dracula? He must have been a good actor.

"I'd like to introduce you to your biggest fan," Aunt Libby told him.

My mind was still on the figure lurking outside. "Aunt Libby, we really should—" I began.

"I've come to suck your blood!" Dracula said in a ghoulish voice, lunging at me.

I had to keep from rolling my eyes.

There was a time not too long ago when meeting an actor who played Dracula in a professional production would have been the highlight of my existence. I would have become a gushy groupie in his presence and kept his framed autograph on my bookshelf. Now it was more like meeting a shopping mall Easter Bunny.

"Libby has told me so much about you," Dracula continued.

"Nice to meet you," I said. "We were just—"

"Come, sit down," Aunt Libby suggested, offering a

folding chair to the ghoulish lead.

"Your aunt tells me you are obsessed with vampires," he said, draping his cape over the chair and sitting down.

Actually, I'm dating one, I wanted to say.

"Have you been to the Coffin Club?" he asked me.

"She's too young," Aunt Libby reminded him as she sat in her dressing-room chair and began taking off her makeup.

"Have *you*?" I asked eagerly.

"Yes. For research purposes only."

"Did you see anything unusual?" I inquired, like a gothic Nancy Drew.

"Everything there is unusual." He laughed. "Kids walk around wearing medieval cloaks and vampire teeth, with metal spears piercing through their eyebrows and lips, and amulets of blood hanging from their necks. I think I was the only one there above thirty. Except for one other man."

"Older than you?"

"Well, stranger, if you can imagine."

"I didn't mean—"

"I know. He stuck out, too. But not in the way I did. He could have played Renfield."

"Creepy Man?" I blurted out. "I mean, was he creepy?"

"Well, I guess he was."

Unfortunately it must have been this dime-store Dracula, and not Alexander, whom Elvira had spotted talking with Jameson.

"He was quite eccentric," Marshall continued. "He

asked if I was aware of any abandoned mansions in the area. Dark, secluded, near a cemetery, with an attic."

"Are there any? I love old mansions."

"I confessed I was starring in *Dracula*," Marshall said proudly, "and I'd been to the Historical Society to research mansions and local cemeteries. I explained to him that he was better off going to the Historical Society than a real estate agent."

Dracula got up to leave. "It was a pleasure meeting you."

I could still see the figure creeping outside through the partially covered window. When I turned to look at Aunt Libby as she thanked Marshall for his visit, I could see their reflections in the long mirror, as well as the reflection of the window through which I'd been peering. The alley appeared empty. But when I turned back to the window, the figure was still there.

Alexander?

I quickly headed for the door, pushing past the exiting Dracula.

"Raven," Aunt Libby scolded.

"I'm sorry," I began. "I think I saw one of your fans outside. I'm going to see if they want to meet you!"

I rushed outside, past a smelly Dumpster, some discarded antique chairs, and stage scenery. Fire escapes hung from overhead.

When I came to the other side of the dressing-room window, the figure had already gone.

Disappointed, I looked around for any signs. The alley was empty of people. A glistening object on the cracked blacktop underneath the window caught my eye.

On closer inspection, I saw a pewter skeleton earring lying next to a puddle. I'd vaguely remembered seeing someone wearing an earring just like this. But Alexander wore studs. Then it hit me—it had been Jagger.

I checked all around me, making sure the coast was clear. I picked it up, stuck the earring in my purse, and ran back inside the theater.

Aunt Libby and I walked to her car with some of the other cast members. With each step, I couldn't help but feel as if someone was watching me.

I looked up and spotted a small dark object dangling from the telephone wire above the alley.

"Is that a bat?" I asked as she unlocked my door.

"I can't see anything," she said.

"Over there." I pointed.

Aunt Libby squinted. "I'm sure it's a bird," she commented.

"Birds don't hang upside down," I said.

"You're creeping me out!" she hollered, and swiftly raced around to her side and got into the Beetle.

Could it be Alexander? Or were my suspicions right about Jagger?

As my aunt started the car, I looked back at the wire, which was now bare.

"What are you doing?" Aunt Libby asked, back at her bachelorette pad, as I turned on all the lights. "Are you paying for the electric bill this month?"

She followed behind, turning them off.

"We have to keep them on," I declared.

"All of them?"

"Didn't my dad tell you? I'm afraid of the dark."

She glared at me in disbelief. "This from a girl who has sleepovers at cemeteries?"

She had a point. But I couldn't tell her my most secretest of all secrets. "The show really spooked me," I said instead. "You gave such a realistic performance, I'm afraid I could be bitten at any moment."

"You thought I was that believable?" she asked, surprised.

I nodded eagerly.

"Well, I prefer candlelight," she said. She lit some votives and placed them throughout the living room. Her apartment began to smell of roses and flickered with shadows of Italian masks.

Had I really met a second teen vampire? Maybe Jagger had been afraid I'd spotted his unreflected image in my compact. He might have been spying on me in the alleyway, or watching me as he hung from a telephone wire. I took a deep breath, realizing I was no better than an overreacting gossipmonger like Trevor Mitchell. I should be spending my time planning my continuing search for Alexander instead of pointing fingers to a white-haired goth's mortal existence. Jagger could have dropped his earring on his way home from the Coffin Club. The lurking figure could have been a clubster, weaving back and forth by the Dumpster after having a few too many Executions.

I picked up Aunt Libby's Lava lamp phone and called my parents.

"Hello?" Billy Boy answered.

"It's me. Are Mom and Dad home?"

"They're next door, visiting the Jenkins's new baby," he replied.

"They left you alone?" I asked, ribbing him.

"Give it a rest."

"Well, don't touch my room! Or anything in it," I warned, wrapping the telephone cord around my fingers.

"I've already read one of your journals."

"You better be kidding!"

"'Alexander kissed me!'" he said in a girlish voice. Then I heard him leaf through pages.

"You better—"

"'Trevor was right,'" he continued. "'Alexander really is a vampire.'"

I froze. How had Billy Boy gotten hold of one of my journals?

"Close it right now!" I cried. "It's not a journal. It's a story I'm writing for English class!"

"Well, you have a lot of spelling mistakes."

"Right now, Nerd Boy! Shut it or I'm coming home and melting all your computer games!"

"Calm down, spaz. I'm in my room, leafing through my NASA book," he confessed. "You think I want to go in your messy room? I could be missing for days!"

"I knew that," I said, with a sigh of relief. "Well, tell Mom I called." I was amazed how accurately Billy Boy had guessed the contents of my journal. Maybe he should perform crystal-ball readings at the Coffin Club.

"Oh, someone called for you," he remembered.

"Becky?"

"No. It was a guy."

I held my breath. "Alexander?"

"He didn't leave his name. When I said you weren't home, he hung up."

"Did you check the caller ID?"

I waited an eternity for his response.

"Out of area," he finally answered.

"If he calls again, ask who it is," I demanded. "And then call me immediately!"

Aunt Libby was munching on carrots dipped in hummus while sitting on the floor on a purple corduroy pillow. I was too distraught to eat.

"So tell me about your boyfriend," she asked, as if reading my thoughts.

"Well, he's a goth like me," I answered, beginning to tell her the part of Alexander's identity that wasn't secret. "And he's delicious!"

"What does he look like?"

"Luscious, long midnight hair. Deep, dreamy eyes. He's taller than me, about your height. Thin, not malnourished, but not beefy like he has to be in a gym twenty-four-seven. I just can't believe he left," I added, remembering the farewell note.

"He left you?"

"No, I mean he left for spring break." I scrambled, trying to cover my mistake. "To visit his family."

"I'm glad you found someone special you can identify

53

with. It must be hard for you growing up in that town."

I appreciated that Libby understood what it was like to be different. Because she felt more comfortable in Hipsterville, maybe Alexander had found a place where he felt more comfortable, too.

"Aunt Libby, can I ask you a personal question?"

"Of course."

"Do you believe in vampires?"

She laughed. "I thought you were going to ask about sex."

But I was serious. "Do you?"

"I once dated a guy who kept a vial around his neck. He claimed it was blood, but it smelled like strawberry Kool-Aid."

"Did he creep you out?"

"Actually the ones who claimed they weren't vampires scared me more," she teased. "We should get some sleep. We've both had a long day," she said, blowing the votives out and putting the carrots away. "I'm so glad you're here," she said, giving me a squeeze.

"Me, too."

As soon as Aunt Libby went into her bedroom, I tiptoed through the apartment and turned the other lights back on, just to be safe. I climbed onto the futon, pulled the covers over me, and closed my eyes.

Suddenly I felt a shadow on me. I squeezed my eyes shut. I imagined Alexander standing over me with flowers, begging my forgiveness for leaving so abruptly. But then I realized it could be Jagger, about to plunge his fangs into my neck.

I opened my eyes slowly.

"Aunt Libby!" I shouted with relief.

"Still spooked?" she asked, standing over me. "You can leave the living room light on."

Libby turned all the other lights off and returned to her bedroom, unaware I was trying to protect her from a tattooed teen of darkness. I pulled the covers back over my head, but still felt as if someone were watching me. I tried to calm myself by thinking of Alexander. I recalled lying in the grass with him, in the backyard of the Mansion, staring at the stars, our fingers intertwined.

I heard a scratching sound coming from the kitchen. I was probably the only girl in the world who hears a scratching sound and hopes it's a mouse. I imagined myself back at the Mansion, the dark sky brightened by luminous clouds above us, the smell of Drakar cologne in the air, and Alexander kissing me. But when Alexander spoke into my ear, all I heard was that scratching sound.

I decided to confront it and walked toward the kitchen in my black socks. A white mouse running across my feet was the least of my issues.

I switched on the kitchen light. The sound seemed to be coming from outside.

I peeled back the curtain above the sink, expecting to see Jagger's ghost-white face staring back. But it was only a tree branch swaying against the window in the wind.

Just to be safe, I opened my Tupperware container and placed a clove of garlic on the windowsill above the futon. ·

7

The Historical Society

The next morning, I was jarred awake by the music of the Doors. The bright sun beaming in through the open windows made my head pound. I was exhausted from the bus ride to Hipsterville, searching for Alexander, and my nocturnal meeting with the inhabitants of the Coffin Club. As I looked outside, the mortal world seemed the same. Jeeps parallel parked. Hipstervillians pushed chic strollers. Birds hung on telephone wires.

But the morning sun shed new light on last night's events. Maybe my Coffin Club experience was just a dream and Jagger just a concoction of my nighttime imagination.

I rose from the futon with a gentle laugh, thinking about my overimaginative nocturnal dreams, when I spotted a charm on Aunt Libby's wooden footlocker, next to my bracelets.

Jagger's skeleton earring. It hadn't been a dream.

I held it in my hand. The bony charm stared up at me.

If Jagger was a vampire, I wondered what frights it had observed, dangling from his ear. Was it witness to late-night bites on unsuspecting girls? Had the tiny pewter bones seen Alexander?

I reminded myself that I was doing to Jagger what Trevor had done to Alexander. Trevor had started rumors that the Sterlings were vampires, not because he knew their true identity, but because he wanted to make them a town scandal. Now I was making judgments and jumping to my own conclusions about Jagger without having any facts. I had to spend my energies searching for what I had come to Hipsterville for—a real vampire instead of a wannabe.

I remembered my conversation with the Village Dracula. I had to get to the Historical Society as soon as it opened.

I found Aunt Libby in the kitchen cooking eggs.

"Good morning, honey," she said. "Did you sleep well?"

"Like a baby."

"I'm surprised you did," she said, cutting me off. "Something in the living room smells funny," she said, turning off the stove and placing the skillet on another burner.

"My mom packed me some goodies for the bus ride," I said, following her into the living room. "Maybe something spoiled."

"It seems like it's coming from over here," she said, pointing toward the window above the futon.

She quickly pulled back a broken window shade before I could stop her.

"I found it on the floor last night when I went to the bathroom," I improvised. "I thought it was a seashell."

I paused, waiting for her response.

She looked at me skeptically.

"Well, after watching your show last night, I just couldn't sleep," I added.

"But I thought you liked vampires."

"I do, but not at my window."

"You remind me of your father when he was growing up. Loved scary movies, but must have slept with the light on until college," she said.

"Then I guess it's in my genes," I said, retrieving the garlic from the windowsill and sticking it back in the Tupperware container.

"I can throw that away for you," she offered, extending her hand.

"I want to keep it," I said, as I put the container in my purse. "Until college."

Aunt Libby laughed, and I followed her into the kitchen. "I have a list of things we can do," she said, as we sat down to breakfast. "We can start by going to the art museum. There's an exhibition on Edward Gorey I think you might enjoy. We can go to the Nifty Fifties diner for lunch; they make a great bacon cheeseburger. Of course, I've never had it, but that's what I hear. After that, we can go antiquing in the neighborhood. Then I have my show. But you can hang backstage. I'm afraid it might be too scary for you to see again," she teased. "Sound cool?"

"I'd like to check out the Historical Society," I requested.

"All that talk about mansions last night with Marshall?" she guessed.

"I think I'll do a report on one for history class."

"During spring break? I figured you'd rather have a picnic in the cemetery," she said, putting down her coffee.

"Great idea! Let's do that afterward."

"I was joking," she responded.

By the time Aunt Libby got ready and I showered and dressed, the morning hours were dwindling. Libby was everything my dad wasn't—while he was an uptight type-A personality, she was a laid-back type-ZZZ. He was fifteen minutes early to a movie, and she was lucky to make it before the credits rolled.

I couldn't convince Aunt Libby to pack a basket of tortilla-wrapped tofu sandwiches and sit by empty graves, but I was able to trade in the art museum for the Historical Society. I grabbed my Olivia Outcast journal from my suitcase and put it in my backpack, and we finally headed out the door.

Dullsville's Historical Society was in an unhaunted late-nineteenth-century church. I had visited it only once on a school field trip and spent most of the time exploring the three tombstones in the cemetery until a teacher discovered my whereabouts and threatened to call my parents.

Hipsterville's Historical Society proved to be more interesting, located in two Pullman railway cars at the old train station.

Inside, I rummaged through pictures of Victorian houses, original menus from Joe's Eats, and letters from early residents. From the second car emerged a woman wearing a lime green pantsuit with matching sandals and a red-hair *That Girl* do.

"Can I help you?" she asked.

"My niece is visiting and would like to do a report on our historical mansions," Aunt Libby said, peering at black-and-white photos of streetcars that hung next to the emergency brake.

"Well, you came to the right place," she said, and pulled a book from a shelf.

"I'm interested in an abandoned estate near a cemetery."

The woman looked at me as if I were a ghost. "Strange. A man was in here the other day asking about the very same thing!"

"Really?" I asked, surprised.

"Was it Marshall Kenner?" Aunt Libby inquired. "He's starring in *Dracula*."

"No, Marshall was in earlier in the month. This was a gentleman who was new to town."

My ears perked up.

She pulled out several more books and leafed through them as Aunt Libby explored the museum.

"Here's the Landford Mansion," the woman pointed out. "It's in the far north part of town. And the Kensley Estate, toward the east."

I studied all the pictures, imagining which one Jameson would have selected. Nothing remotely resembled the Mansion on Benson Hill.

"Which one was the man interested in?" I whispered.

She looked at me strangely. "You should do your report on what *you* like."

I looked again at all the mansions, each one statelier than the last. I wrote down their names and addresses on the back of the Historical Society's brochure and realized it would take me several spring breaks to visit them all.

As I was ready to close the book, I noticed the edge of a bookmark peeking out toward the back. When I turned to the noted page, I lost my breath. A black-and-white photo of a gloomy nineteenth-century grand estate stared back at me. A wrought-iron gate surrounded the towering house, and at the top of the mansion was a tiny attic window. I envisioned ghosts hiding behind the curtains, too shy to be photographed.

Underneath, the picture read "Coswell Manor House."

"What's this?" I asked the woman, who was organizing the bookshelf.

She glanced at the picture. "I didn't think to mention that one because it's on the outskirts of town. It's been abandoned for years."

"It's perfect," I said.

"Weird. That's what that gentleman said, too."

The woman jotted down an address and handed it to me. "It's on Lennox Hill at the far end of the road."

I dropped a donation in the "Friendly Funds" jar as we left the museum.

"That was nice of you," my aunt said, as we walked through the parking lot to the Nifty Fifties diner.

"I'd have given her my college fund if I could've."

In a Manor of Speaking 8

Whille Aunt Libby gathered her belongings for the
theater and the sun made its final descent, I sat
cross-legged on her futon and made notes in my journal.

My investigation was almost complete. In only a few
hours, I would be reunited with Alexander. Once he understood I loved him no matter who or what he was, we could
go back to Dullsville and we'd be able to be together.

Then I wondered what exactly that would mean.
Would he want me to be like him in every way I could?
And if faced with the choice, would I really want to
choose the lifestyle I'd always dreamed of?

To quiet my mind, I made more notes:

Positives of Being a Vampire
1. Save on electric bills.
2. Could always sleep in late—very late.

3. Wouldn't have to worry about keeping a low-carb diet.

"Are you sure you want to stay alone?" Aunt Libby asked, holding her makeup bag.

"I am sixteen."

"Your parents let you stay by yourself?"

"I could have been babysitting at twelve, if anyone in Dullsville would have hired me."

"Well, there's plenty of food in the fridge," she offered, heading for the door. "I'll call at intermission to check in."

Aunt Libby may have been laid back when it came to her own lifestyle, but when I was under her roof she was just like my dad. I guess she would have been like my father and left her hippie days behind if she had had kids, too.

I quickly changed into my Hot Gothics fashion merch—black-and-white-striped tights and a torn black minidress revealing a blood-red chemise. I applied my standard black lipstick and dark eye shadow. I barely had enough time to put a red rose body tattoo on my neck.

I checked to make sure the container of garlic was tightly sealed, as I didn't want to expose Alexander to the two-inch weapon I'd use to ward off any lurking vampires. I must have brushed my hair and rearranged my red extensions a million times before I rushed out the door and waited at the bus stop for the number seven.

With every passing number eleven or sixteen, I paced the bus stop. I was considering returning to my aunt's apartment and calling a cab when I saw the number seven turn onto the street and slowly lumber toward me. Anxiously, I boarded the crowded bus, a mixture of granola heads and urbanites, slipped my cash into the change receptacle, and grabbed the slippery aluminum pole. I held on to the pole for dear life, trying to keep my balance and avoid bumping into the other passengers as the bus jolted with every acceleration. As soon as the number seven lurched forward and reached the speed limit, it began to slow down again, stopping at every bus stop in town. I checked my watch. It would have been quicker if I'd walked.

After letting off a few dozen passengers and picking up a few more, the bus driver turned the corner and passed my destination—Lennox Hill Road.

I ran toward the front of the bus.

"You passed Lennox Hill Road!" I called in a panic as the bus driver continued accelerating.

"There is no bus stop there," he said to me, looking in his rearview mirror.

"But that's my destination," I argued.

"I only stop at bus stops," he recited, continuing to drive.

"If it's a dollar fifty to get on the bus, how much is it to get off?"

I heard a few of the passengers laugh behind me.

"Pull the cord," the woman said, pointing to a white wire that ran above the bus windows.

I reached across her and pulled the wire hard.

A few seconds later, the bus driver slowed down and pulled over.

"See that?" he asked, pointing to a square sign on a pole with the number seven next to the curb. "That's a bus stop."

I gave him a dirty look and jumped off the bus, dodging an elderly couple trying to board. I ran down the road the bus had just driven up until I reached Lennox Hill Road. I turned the corner and walked past gigantic pristine estates with lush green lawns and purple and yellow flowers until I found an unkempt, overgrown weed-filled lawn. A decaying house sat on it at the end of a cold and ominous cul-de-sac. It looked as if a storm cloud were hovering over it. I had finally arrived at the stately gothic manor house.

Gargoyles sat on top of the jagged wrought-iron gates. Untamed bushes lined the front of the manor. The dead grass crunched beneath my boots. A broken birdbath sat in the center of the lawn. Moss and ivy grew on the roof like a gothic Chia Pet. I skipped along a fractured rock path, which led to an arched wooden front door.

I grabbed on the dragon-shaped knocker, and it came off the door and fell into my hand. Embarrassed, I quickly hid the knocker underneath a bush.

I rapped the door again. I wondered if Alexander was standing on the other side, ready to greet me with a colossal kiss. But there was no answer. I banged my fist against the door until my hand began to throb.

I turned the rusty handle and tried to push against the wooden entrance, but it was locked.

I snuck behind the dead bushes alongside the front of the manor. The windows were boarded up, but I spotted a slender crack. The ceilings in the manor house were so high, I was surprised that there were no clouds wafting through the rafters—plenty of room for a ghost to fly around in without even being noticed. From what I could see, the walls in the living room were as bare as the room itself.

Frustrated, I walked around to the side of the manor house and discovered a butler's entrance. I twisted the iron knob on the skinny oak door, but that, too, was bolted shut.

My heart pulsing hard, I ran to the back of the house. A few broken steps led down to a lone dingy window. It wasn't boarded up, so I eagerly pressed my face to the glass.

Nothing unusual. I saw a few cardboard boxes, a dusty tool rack, and an old sewing machine.

I tried to open the window, but it was stuck. I ran back up the broken steps and stood on the lawn.

"Hello?" I called. "Jameson? Alexander?"

But my words were answered only by the barking of a neighbor's dog.

I stared up at a single attic window. A tree starved of leaves leaned toward the manor house, one of its branches reaching out just below the window. The huge oak must have been centuries old—its trunk was as wide as a house, and its roots clutched the ground like a spider's legs. I was used to climbing, whether it was over the Mansion's wrought-iron gate or up apple trees in Becky's backyard. But scaling this tree seemed like ascending Mt. Everest in the dark. Clad in combat boots and a minidress, I stuck my heel onto the lowest branch and pulled myself up. I continued to climb at a steady rate, slowing down only to catch my breath or when I needed to feel above me for a limb hiding away from the moonlight. Weary but determined, I scooted along a heavy branch stretching underneath the attic window.

A dark curtain hid most of the room from view, but I managed to peek inside. I could make out an empty box and a wooden chair. Then, I saw the most amazing sight staring back at me—resting in the corner was the portrait Alexander had painted of me dressed for the Snow Ball. A pumpkin basket hung over one arm. A two-dimensional Raven grinned, flashing fake vampire teeth.

"Alexander!" I called. I tried to tap against the window, but my fingers were just out of reach.

"Alexander!" I called again.

I could hear the dog's bark getting louder.

"Alexander! Jameson!" I yelled with all my might.

Just then, the next-door neighbor opened his back door and stepped onto his deck. He was built like a professional wrestler.

"Hey! You kids back again?" he called over.

"What's going on, Hal?" a petite woman asked, following him out of the house.

"I told you, kids are playing in that house next door," he said to her. "I'm calling the police!" he yelled, and pulled out a cell phone from his back pocket.

I scurried down the tree, wanting to avoid being placed in a full nelson or, worse, handcuffs. Plus, I didn't want law enforcement to arrest Alexander and Jameson or force them to find another home—and this time it might be Romania.

When I reached the bottom branch, I saw, out of the corner of my eye, a rustling of the dark curtain in the attic window.

I quickly stepped back to get a better view.

But the curtain was still.

Suddenly, a chocolate-colored Doberman pinscher sprinted out of the neighbor's house, down the deck stairs, and scratched against the brown picket fence that ran parallel to the manor house.

Afraid the dog would wriggle his way through the skinny spaces between the boards and devour me like Kibbles 'n Bits, I took off around the other side of the manor and tore down the road to the bus stop.

I boarded the westbound number seven, taking a seat in the back behind a college-aged couple. I was excited to find that Alexander was indeed in Hipsterville. I imagined that he was painting portraits in a spooky cemetery. Searching a haunted mansion for furniture to decorate his attic room. Or maybe he was out for a night flight.

I was still confused why Alexander had come to Hipsterville. It was a small town with eerie abandoned manors, and with enough goths and artists to be hidden among. What else did it offer a lone vampire?

The couple seated in front of me began making out, oblivious to the other staring passengers.

I saw their reflections in the bus window. I wondered if they knew how lucky they were. Two humans who could share their nights and days together. Take pictures. Sit in the sun. Then I realized those were just small sacrifices I'd make to be with Alexander again.

The bus approached the Village Players Theater, and I disembarked with several other passengers. I walked alone down the alley toward the back entrance of the theater, conjuring excuses I could tell Aunt Libby and my parents so I could stake out the manor house for the next few nights until I made contact with Alexander. I saw a figure lurking behind the Dumpster.

"I hoped to find you here," a deep voice said, stepping out to block my way.

I froze. It was Jagger. I held my purse close; inside was my Mace and, possibly more important, my container of garlic.

"I have information that may be of interest to you."

"Information?" I asked skeptically.

"About Sterling," he said, with a knowing glance. "Isn't that who you are looking for?"

Shocked, I inched back. I knew where Alexander was staying, but I didn't know where he was. The promise of any new leads on Alexander's whereabouts made my heart pulse in overtime. Plus, my curiosity about Jagger's identity still lingered. I had to know how he knew Alexander.

"I can help you. I've known him for an eternity," he said with a grin.

I glanced back at the Village Players Theater. If I went back inside, I was guaranteed to have a safe night with real unreal vampires. Or I could just wait for Alexander outside the manor house—unless he and Jameson spotted me and left for another town. Then I was guaranteed to never see my Gothic Mate again.

"You better tell me everything you know," I said, clutching my purse to my side. "Otherwise—"

"You are free to go whenever you like," he reassured me.

I stood still as Jagger began walking down the alley.

Curiosity eating away at me, I decided to catch up to him. I followed Jagger down the street and toward a back entrance to the Coffin Club.

He led me into the warehouse and down a darkened hallway to an empty freight elevator. The rickety door shrieked out in pain when he shut it. Instead of pushing the button for the Coffin Club, he pressed the "B" button.

The elevator slowly lowered to the basement, screeching as if it were a coffin descending into hell.

"I thought we were going to the Coffin Club."

The elevator stopped. Jagger opened the door and held it for me as I stepped into a corridor.

He followed behind me so closely I could feel his warm breath on the back of my neck. We walked down the narrow hallway, the walls adorned with graffiti and the cement floor cluttered with discarded chairs and boxes. The dance floor music pulsed above. When we reached what looked like a wide storage-room door, I could hear the elevator slowly grind its way back up to mortal level. Jagger lifted the metal-gray door above our heads to reveal a windowless apartment.

I stepped inside.

"Welcome to my dungeon," he said.

Dozens of medieval candelabras filled the spacious apartment.

And then I saw it. In the far corner lay an open coffin, adorned with gothic band stickers like a mortal teen's skateboard. Dirt encircled the coffin like a walled city.

My eyes grew wide. "So you are. . . ," I began, but could barely speak.

"Oh, the coffin," he said. "Cool, huh? I got it at a vintage store."

"And the dirt?"

"Saw it in a vampire mag. Creepy, huh?"

I didn't know what to think. Even Alexander slept on a mattress.

"It's really comfortable. Want to give it a try?" he asked with sexy eyes.

"I'm not tired."

"You don't have to be."

Jagger confused me. I couldn't figure out if he was a vulpine vampire or just a goth-obsessed teen like me.

I looked around for any other unusual clues—but everything was unusual. Maps were spread out on the floor. The cement walls were decorated with gravestone etchings.

Next to the radiator an aquarium, without water, was filled with rocks.

His kitchen counter and sink looked as if they had remained untouched. Metal cabinets were missing their doors. I was afraid to think what was in the refrigerator—or, rather, who.

"You are the first girl I've ever brought down here," Jagger confessed.

"I'm surprised. You must meet a lot of girls at the Coffin Club."

"Actually, I'm new to town. Just like you. Visiting."

The hairs on the back of my neck rose. "How do you know I'm visiting?"

"It doesn't take a psychic to figure it out. Someone as

goth as you would be a regular at the club. Romeo had never seen you before."

"Uh . . . I guess you're right."

"Can I get you anything to drink?"

"No, thank you," I replied. "I want to know—"

Jagger walked over to the aquarium. He placed his hand inside and pulled out a huge tarantula.

"I just bought him. Would you like to pet him?" he asked, stroking the potentially poisonous spider as if it were a sleeping cat.

Normally I would have loved to pet a tarantula, but I wasn't sure of Jagger's motive.

"Where's your big-screen TV?" I asked, noticing the lack of televisions or computers.

"I find them offensive."

"So you don't watch movies? You've never even seen the original *Dracula*?" I hinted. "*Nosferatu*? *Kissing Coffins*? Someone as goth as you would seem to have the lines memorized."

"I would rather experience life than be a voyeur."

He returned the spider to the aquarium. I dug my hand into my purse.

"You left this behind," I said, and revealed the skeleton earring in my hand. He smiled brightly as if I were reuniting him with a long-lost friend.

As he took the charm from my hand, his fingers lingered, gently touching my palm, sending chills through my veins. It took some strength, but I withdrew.

"Now that this has been in your possession, it is even more special to me," he said, placing it back in his ear.

"Can I give you a reward?" he asked.

"You can tell me about Alexander."

"Shall I tell you? Or should I just show you," he asked, stepping toward me.

"Tell me," I said, defiant. "Is he a friend of yours?"

"Maybe yes," he said with an inviting smile. "Maybe no," he said with a wicked grin.

"Forget it, I'm outta here."

"I know him from Romania," he said quickly.

"Have you seen him in America?"

He shook his head, his white hair flopping over his blue and green eyes.

"Do you know where he is?" I asked.

"What if I do? How much is it worth?" he asked, licking his lips.

"You don't know, do you?" I challenged. I backed away from him, stepping on a map.

"But you know quite a lot," he argued.

I pulled my purse close.

"You knew enough about my Romanian friend to come to the Coffin Club and ask for him," he said, approaching me again.

"I don't know anything—"

"Then why do you want to find him?" he whispered softly in my ear as he gently stroked my hair off my shoulder.

"I must have been mistaken—" I said, looking away from his gaze, wanting to run, but not being able to move.

"Really?" he whispered. "He made you feel like his breath was yours," he said, circling me, his words landing

73

softly on the back of my neck.

"I don't know what you are talking about," I lied, my heart pounding in my chest.

"That your flesh and his are one," he said, as his lips gently caressed the nape of my neck.

I could barely speak, my heart racing, the map crinkling underneath my boot.

He stepped close in front of me, his eyes piercing through my own, and gently touched my onyx necklace.

He leaned into me and kissed the top of my chest. He whispered, "That you are just a kiss away from being bonded with him for eternity."

I could barely breathe. My heart raced as he held me.

"Get off!" I cried, wedging my arms between us and pushing him away.

A map tore underneath my boot. Jagger tried to pierce me with his gaze, but I stared down at my feet. It was a map of Hipsterville. The cemeteries were highlighted in yellow, with several crossed out in black marker.

Then I noticed, lying a few feet away on the floor, the other maps—neighboring towns of Hipsterville and Dullsville. Cemeteries were highlighted and crossed out in black.

I glanced up at Jagger as he tried to lock his blue and green eyes with mine. He gently grabbed my hand like he'd done in the Coffin Club. "We can find him together," I recalled him saying. Then I remembered the note I'd found in Alexander's room—"HE IS ON HIS WAY!"

I backed away from Jagger and reached into my purse. It was worth a shot. My fingers shook as I tried to pry open the container of garlic.

The container's suction was like Super Glue. I struggled with the lid when Jagger stepped toward me.

I raced out the door and ran down the hallway. I pressed the elevator button and glanced back. Jagger stepped through his doorway and began running down the hall after me. I could hear the screeching elevator above me, but it was nowhere to be found. I looked up. The number "3" lit up; "2" lit up. "G" lit.

"Hurry! Hurry!" I mumbled, pressing the button repeatedly.

I could hear Jagger coming closer. Suddenly the "B" lit up, and the elevator stopped in front of me. I pulled the rickety door to one side and jumped in. I used all my strength to pull the accordion door shut just as an angry Jagger stepped in front of the elevator.

I darted back, away from the door, as his gaze caught me. He reached out for the door, realizing I hadn't yet pushed a button. I quickly pressed my finger against the "G" button.

As the elevator began to lift, I leaned against the wall, away from him. "I hope you find him," I heard Jagger call. "Before I do."

"What are you doing here?" Aunt Libby asked when she found me peeking underneath the shades in her dressing room after curtain call. "I called you at intermission, but you didn't pick up."

"I must have been in the shower," I rambled. "But I wanted to see you."

"You did? That's so cute!" she said, wiping off her makeup.

"I'm having such a fabulous time. But I have something to tell you."

"Yes?"

"I have to go back home tomorrow."

"So soon?" she asked, putting down her makeup sponge.

"I know," I whined. "I don't want to leave, but I still have tons of homework to do."

"When I was in school, spring break was just that—a break."

"And I'll need to leave early. Before sunset."

"Still afraid of the vampires?" she teased.

The truth was, I wasn't sure—I didn't know who or what Jagger was. The one thing I was sure of was that he was following Alexander.

It was just moments ago that I had barely escaped Jagger's lair. If I attempted to find out Jagger's reason for his search, I might be putting myself—and, more important, Alexander—in danger.

Now that Jagger was following me—outside the theater yesterday and waiting for me in the alley tonight—I knew if I returned to the manor house, or anywhere I thought I might find Alexander, I would lead Jagger right to him. Although it broke my heart, I had no choice. I would have to leave Hipsterville.

Aunt Libby and I sat together on a wooden bench outside the Greyhound bus station waiting for the eight
o'clock to pull in. There was only one bus each day out of
Hipsterville, and it departed just as the sun was setting.

I looked forward to returning to Dullsville and hopefully Alexander, but I was sad to leave Aunt Libby. I
enjoyed our visit together, and I really admired her. She had
followed her dream of being an actress and in the process
lived independently, with her own style, tastes, and view of
life. She saw me as unique and special, instead of as a freak.
And most important, she treated me like I was normal.

I'd also miss the excitement of Hipsterville, knowing
there was a place like the Coffin Club for goths to hang
out and dance, and Hipsterville's Hot Gothics—a store
where I could purchase gothic clothes, spiked jewelry, and
body tattoos.

Libby put her arm around me, and I leaned my head on her shoulder as the bus pulled in.

"I'm going to miss you so much, Aunt Libby," I said, squeezing her with all my might before I climbed aboard the bus.

As I walked down the aisle, I opened my compact to check the other travelers. After everyone reflected back, even a gothic couple snuggling in back, I chose a seat next to the window. Aunt Libby waved to me as we waited for the bus to leave. I could see in her eyes that she would miss me as much as I'd miss her. She kept waving as the bus drove off. But as soon as the station was out of sight, I breathed a sigh of relief. The nefarious, mysterious, feud-seeking shock-goth Jagger was now behind me. Hopefully, a new plan to contact my handsome Gothic Prince Alexander was before me.

The bus ride back to Dullsville was painfully long. I called Becky from my cell phone, but she was at the movies with Matt. I jotted notes about my encounter with Jagger in my Olivia Outcast journal, but writing gave me motion sickness. I imagined why Jagger was searching for Alexander—maybe it was a feud between the two families over the baroness's Mansion—but it only made me worry about my boyfriend. I dreamed about reuniting with Alexander, but I also couldn't stop thinking about the maps Jagger had lying on his floor.

It seemed like an eternity until the bus finally pulled into Dullsville's bus stop. I even hoped against hope that

Alexander would magically be waiting for me, but instead I was greeted by Mom, Dad, Billy Boy, and his nerd-mate Henry.

"You're leaving already?" my dad asked after we arrived back home and I dropped my suitcase off in my room. "We want to hear more about your trip."

I didn't have time for my parents' well-meaning questions. "How did you like Aunt Libby? What did you think of her performance in *Dracula*? Did you like eating tofu sandwiches?"

I wanted to go to the place where I did my best thinking.

"I have to see Alexander!" I said, shutting the front door behind me.

I raced to the Mansion and found the iron gate ajar. Out of breath, I hurried up the long, winding driveway and noticed something peculiar—the front door was also ajar.

Maybe he'd seen me from the manor house attic window and followed me back to Dullsville.

"Alexander?" I called as I walked inside.

The entranceway, living room, and dining room were as I'd last seen them, covered and empty of paintings.

"Alexander?" I called, walking up the grand staircase. My heart beat wildly with each step.

I whisked through the second floor and up Alexander's attic steps. I reached his bedroom. I could barely breathe. I gently knocked on his door. "Alexander, it's me, Raven."

No one responded.

I turned the knob and opened the door. This room also looked like I'd last seen it, bare except for a few remaining items. But on his unmade bed lay a backpack. *He had come back.*

I picked up the rustic black bag and hugged it. I knew it would be rude to look through the backpack, especially if Alexander suddenly walked into the room. But I couldn't help it.

I sat it back on the bed and began to unzip it when I heard a noise coming from the backyard.

I looked outside his attic window and saw a candle flickering in the gazebo. A bat was hovering above the roof.

I took off, bolting out of his room, down the attic stairs, around the second floor, and down the never-ending staircase.

I flew out the front door and raced around to the backyard.

"Alexander!" I called, and ran into the darkened gazebo, barely able to make out his features in the shadows.

Then the candlelight flickered. I saw his eyes first. One green and one blue, before he stepped fully into the moonlight.

I tried to run, but it was too late. Jagger's gaze had already begun to make me dizzy.

I awoke on my back, on cold wet grass, with raindrops kissing my face, as if in a Sleeping Beauty slumber. The silvery sky held a bright, shining moon. A spidery tree loomed over me, its skinny, naked branches reaching toward me with witch-like fingers.

I sat up, my head aching. Then I saw it. A tombstone. Then another. Not one, but hundreds. I saw the baroness's monument. I was in Dullsville's cemetery.

As I rose, I felt light-headed. I caught my balance on a graveyard marker. I used to seek comfort among the tombstones, but because I was unsure of how I got here, I was anxious to leave before I ended up in an unmarked grave.

Jagger, wearing black cargo pants with red seams and a white T-shirt emblazoned with the words THE PUNISHER, was standing before me.

"How did you get here? Did you follow my bus?" I asked, confused.

"It will all be over in just a few minutes."

"What—my life? Forget it. I'm getting outta here!"

"Not so fast." Jagger grabbed my hand and began leading me toward the middle of the cemetery. I tried to pull away from him, but his grip was too strong and my strength had been depleted from whatever means he used to get me there.

I'd snuck into Dullsville's cemetery many times, and invariably Old Jim, the caretaker, and Luke, his Great Dane, would chase me out. They seemed to be nowhere, now when my life depended on them.

"I thought you were looking for Alexander," I said, but Jagger ignored me and continued pulling me toward the monuments and tombs. We stopped at a closed coffin laid upon a cement bench. I could hear strange music, a mixture of wailing violins and an underlying harpsichord, coming from one of the tombs. On the coffin, a candelabra flickered among the raindrops, wax dripping down its pewter spine. A medieval goblet sat next to it.

It looked like a scene from a gothic wedding.

"What's this?" I asked, my mental fog beginning to wear off.

"A covenant ceremony."

"But where are the guests? I didn't bring a gift," I said, giddy from my daze.

"The bride doesn't have to."

"Bride? But I didn't even register yet!"

Jagger didn't smile. Instead he relit a candle.

A few feet away, I spotted a shovel lying next to an

empty grave, glistening in the moonlight. I backed up slowly, inching my way to the shovel until the caretaker's tool lay at my feet.

My heart was beating so loudly, I was afraid Jagger would hear it. I took a deep breath. As he centered the candelabra on the coffin, I bent over and reached for the handle. But as soon as I grabbed it, Jagger's boot pinned it to the earth. He stood over me as I tried in vain to pry it from the ground. In the struggle, the shiny new shovel shook, and a few bits of clinging dirt fell off the metal head. I saw myself in the shovel's curve, upside down like a spoon's reflection. However, I didn't see a reflection for Jagger right behind me. I looked back up at him. He smiled a wicked smile. I hastily wiped the shovel with my sleeve and shifted to one side, peering into the shiny metal surface. All I could see were the stars above him, but his boot remained on the handle behind me.

I gasped.

"Something missing?" he teased.

I rose quickly and stepped back. "You—" I began, breathless.

I tried to run, but Jagger lunged forward and grabbed my arm. He flashed his fangs at me and licked his lips.

My reality spun out of control. I was standing face-to-face with a real vampire. One who wasn't Alexander. Jagger was the kind I'd read about and seen in movies—the kind who meant to snatch me away from my family and friends and take my blood as his own. I faced pledging my life to a stranger for all eternity. The radical dreams I'd wished for as just a curious goth were about to come true.

But this wasn't my dream. I'd dreamed of eternal love, belonging, and fitting in. Not danger, deceit, and evil. Dullsville hadn't been so dull after Alexander had moved into town. After meeting him, I'd realized all I'd ever wanted was to become one of the living—experiencing movies, metal concerts, and love—and not one of the undead. I wanted to sleep in Alexander's arms, not alone in a coffin. I wanted to turn into a gothic beauty, not a creepy bat. And most important, if I had to make the choice to transform, I would only do it for Alexander.

"My parents are expecting me home. They'll be sending out the SWAT team any minute now."

He held my hand with a strength I'd never felt before. I looked around for anything else to help my escape.

Jagger led me to the front of the coffin. He picked up the goblet and raised it to the moon, spoke a few words in a language I didn't understand, and then took a long drink.

"Now you," he said with a wicked grin, offering me the goblet.

"Forget it!" I said, pushing the goblet away with my free hand.

"But isn't this what you wanted all along? Why else would you follow Alexander?" he asked.

"Because I love him!" I said, trying to wriggle free. "And I will never love you!"

"But you don't have to," he said, and forced the goblet to my mouth.

Drops of thick, sweet liquid spilled against my lips.

I spit the liquid from my mouth. "I will never become like you, whoever or whatever you are!"

Jagger's face grew strange, as if my words had been a silver stake driven through his heart.

"And I say you will!" His blue and green eyes gazed into mine as if trying to cast a spell. "With this kiss, I take thee for all eternity."

Jagger flashed his smile, and his white fangs glistened in the moonlight. He leaned into me.

"I bite back!" I yelled defensively, gritting my teeth.

Suddenly a burst of lightning struck, illuminating the sky and all of the graveyard.

I plunged my teeth into Jagger's arm as hard as I could and dug my nails into his bony hand. He quickly released his death grip. I turned to run but slammed hard into something—or, rather, someone.

"Old Jim?" I cried, confused.

But when I looked up and stared into two midnight eyes, I realized it wasn't the caretaker I'd run into.

Instead, standing before me was my Gothic Guy, like a knight of the night. His dark, shoulder-length hair was hanging in his face. His white, moonlit skin was covered by a black T-shirt and jeans. The plastic spider ring I'd given him was resting on his finger. His eyes were deep, lonely, adoringly intelligent, just as they were the first time I'd seen them.

"Alexander!" I exclaimed, and fell into his arms.

"Just as I thought!" Jagger proclaimed, as if he'd won a contest. "I knew she'd bring me to you!"

Alexander embraced me hard as if he would never release me. Then he pushed me away. "You must go," he commanded.

"Are you crazy? I can't leave you!" I held his hand tightly. "I thought I'd never see you again!"

He stared into my eyes and warned me. "You have to go."

"But I—"

"You shouldn't have brought her into this!" Alexander told Jagger, with an anger I'd never seen before.

"She found *me*. Besides, I'm surprised to see that you're letting her go so soon, after she came all the way to the Coffin Club to find you. . . ."

"Leave Raven out of this!" Alexander exclaimed.

"I couldn't have planned my revenge any better than this. I could destroy you and gain an eternal partner with just one bite."

"You wouldn't dare—" Alexander warned.

"I knew she'd bring you to me, Sterling. You think you're not like one of us, but the truth is you are," Jagger argued.

"What is he talking about?" I asked.

"Not now," Alexander answered.

"Why do you think Sterling left Romania?" Jagger asked me. "Do you think it was an accident he came to a small town in America where there weren't any vampires?"

I didn't really know, after all.

"But I found you, Sterling," Jagger bragged. "And I found Raven."

"She has nothing to do with this," Alexander said,

stepping in between Jagger and me.

"I have nothing to do with what?" I asked curiously.

"Don't worry, Raven, he breaks promises all the time. Right, Sterling?" Jagger said.

Alexander clenched his fist.

"What promise? Why revenge? What does he mean?" I asked, confused, wondering what kind of agreement Alexander had made but couldn't keep.

"Well, I'm not going to leave her! I'm going to hold on to her for all of eternity!" Jagger proclaimed.

He flashed his teeth with a wickedly gnarled grin and leaned in to sink his fangs into my neck.

11

Frightening Farewell

I found myself flat on my back again, wet grass underneath me. Raindrops hit my face. I anxiously felt my neck for any wound.

Alexander leaned over me, his eyes filled with worry.

"Are you okay?" he asked sorrowfully. "You got in the way."

"Am I a . . . ?" I didn't even want to finish my thought.

He shook his head and helped me to my feet. "You have to go!" he commanded again. "You shouldn't be here—you're in danger."

I turned to look around for Jagger. But all I saw were grave markers. "But I may never see you," I pleaded.

"You must leave now," he persisted.

Alexander was breaking my heart again. If I left, it could be for the last time. How could I be sure Jagger wouldn't harm him? Alexander could disappear into the night forever. But if I didn't listen to his instructions, I might actually be doing Alexander more harm by getting in his way.

I saw Jagger stumbling by the baroness's monument and wiping his mouth. His green and blue eyes had turned fiery red. His lean muscles tensed. He grinned at me and licked his lips like a rabid animal ready to rip into its prey.

I didn't even have time to kiss my Gothic Mate good-bye. I ran without looking back, tears and raindrops dripping down my face, the graveyard mud splashing against my boots, my heart pulsing. Thunder clapped against the trees and seemed to echo against the tombstones.

I raced to the entrance of the cemetery and climbed over the fence.

When I turned around, Jagger and Alexander were gone.

12

Risky Reunion

I sobbed as I ran as fast as I could from the cemetery. I could barely see the pavement through my watery eyes. I headed through downtown Dullsville in the pouring rain where drivers in their Saabs, Mercedeses, and Jeeps looked strangely at the sight of a miserable, soaking wet goth girl.

I ran down the main street and tore through shoppers with umbrellas, knocked into couples coming out of the movie theater, and barreled past patrons escaping from the rain into restaurants.

With every flap of a bird's wing or sound of a honking horn, I was startled, thinking it was Jagger following me. I raced on.

I didn't want to go home. I needed to be alone, away from my family. I didn't want to talk—no one, not even Becky, would understand this unearthly experience. I had to hide out and seek comfort in the only place I had ever really felt at home.

I hurried through the open Mansion gates, my legs numb and my feet tingly inside my boots. I rushed up the long, windy driveway and around to the back of the Mansion. I glanced toward the gazebo to see if any two-colored eyeballs were staring back at me. When I found the gazebo empty, I climbed through the open basement window and made my way through the deserted Mansion. My tears dropped onto the creaky wooden floors beneath my squeaky boots. I wiped my eyes as I ascended the grand staircase and made my way into Alexander's attic room.

I touched the empty easel. I gazed at his bed, still creased from when he'd slept there days ago. I held his black knit sweater left behind on his beaten-up comfy chair.

I walked to the attic window and gazed out into the lonely moonlight. The heavy rain had ceased. I felt exhausted, abandoned, like a complete failure. Had I just stayed in Dullsville, Alexander would have returned for me. But my impatience had put me, and Alexander, in danger. He had been safely hiding in Dullsville from Jagger's thirsty revenge, and I'd pointed his nemesis right in his direction. As clever as I thought I was, I'd just been a pawn in Jagger's wicked game.

I heard a floorboard creak behind me. I slowly turned around but could barely make out the dark figure standing in the doorway.

"Jagger—" I said with a gasp.

The floorboard creaked again as the figure took a step toward me.

"Get out!" I yelled, backing up. I had nowhere to go. The figure was blocking the doorway, and my only escape was the narrow attic window ledge.

I stepped away, anxious about making a dangerous escape.

"I'll call the police!" I warned.

The figure drew closer. I decided I'd have to make a run for it by going around him. I took a breath and counted to myself. One. Two. Three.

I speedily darted around the figure, and was close to making my escape through the doorway when the figure grabbed my wrist.

"Get off!" I cried, trying to wriggle away. But when the moonlight gleamed down on his hand, a black plastic spider ring shined back at me.

I gasped, ceasing my struggle. "Alexander?"

He stepped completely into the light.

There he was, like a dream, standing before me. He'd returned. Handsome and now weary looking.

"I thought I'd never see you again!" I exclaimed. My body, tense with fear, melted into him as I wrapped my arms around him. He squeezed me back, so hard I could almost feel his heart beat through my own chest.

"I'm not letting go," I said, squeezing him harder and smiling. "Not ever!"

"I shouldn't have . . ." he began, softly.

I looked up, as if I were seeing an apparition. "I just

can't believe you're here!"

He took my hands and raised them to his mouth, kissing the back of them with his full lips, sending shivers through my veins. He gazed back into my eyes and smiled.

And then he did what I had so longed for him to do. He kissed me. His full lips pressed tenderly against mine, slowly, softly, seductively. It was as if we'd been separated for an eternity.

We continued to kiss, passionately, moving from our mouths to our cheeks to our ears as if drinking in each other's flesh. He gently stroked my hair, then nibbled my ear. I giggled as he sat on his comfy chair and pulled me onto his lap. I looked into his eyes, wondering how I could have breathed the last few days without him near me.

I ran my fingers through his messy, licorice-colored locks.

He brushed my hair away from my neck and made his way up my shoulder with sexy kisses. I could feel his teeth, seductively sliding against the skin of my neck. Touching, toying, tingling, giving me playful nibbles. The nape of my neck hung tenderly in his mouth.

Suddenly Alexander pulled away, a look of terror in his eyes.

"I can't," he said shamefully, looking away.

"What's wrong?" I asked, surprised by his change in mood.

Alexander stood up, helping me to my feet. He anxiously drew his hand through his hair and paced the room.

"It's okay," I said, catching up to him by his easel.

"I thought I wasn't like Jagger," he said, and sat on the

edge of his bed. "But . . . maybe I am."

"You are nothing like him," I said. "In fact, you are the opposite."

"I just want you to be safe. Always," he said, looking at me soulfully.

"I am, now that you are here," I said, stroking his hand.

"But don't you see?" he said seriously. "My world is not a safe one."

"Well, mine isn't either. Don't you watch the news?"

His sullen face turned bright, and he laughed. "I guess you're right."

"See? I'm more at risk going to school with Trevor than I am kissing a vampire."

"I've never met anyone like you," he said, turning toward me. "And I've never felt before the way I feel about you."

"I'm so glad you came back for me." I hugged him around his waist.

"This won't happen again," he assured me.

"How can you be so sure? Jagger seems bent on getting even with you," I asked, sitting beside him.

"Because he couldn't get even."

"Wow, so you showed him who's boss? Like in a school yard brawl?"

"I guess. . . . Only in our case it was a graveyard brawl."

"Is he gone?"

"His family is in Romania. There is nothing for him here now. He can go back and tell them he found me."

I fingered my necklace.

"What promise did you break?"

"I didn't break it. I never made it. . . . But we don't

have to worry about that anymore," he said wearily.

"What were all the candles in the cemetery for?" I asked.

"A vampire can take anyone at any time. But if he takes another at a cemetery or some other sacred ground, then she is his for eternity."

"Then I'm glad you showed up when you did!" I squeezed Alexander with all my might. "I'm sorry I led Jagger to you," I confessed.

"I should be the one apologizing to you. I couldn't imagine you'd come for me," he said, staring off into the moonlight. Then he turned back to me. "But I should have known. That's what I love about you."

"Now tell me everything!" I exclaimed suddenly. "What's it like being a—?"

"What's it like being human?" he interrupted.

"Boring."

"How can you say that?" he asked, holding me close. "You can wake up in the daylight, go to school, and see your reflection."

"But I want to be like you."

"You already are," he said with a smile.

"Were you born a vampire?"

"Yes. Were you born a human?" he teased.

"Yes. Are there millions of vampires around?"

He nodded. "But we are a minority, so we like to stick together. Obviously there is safety in numbers. We can't reveal our identities or we'd be persecuted."

"It must be so hard to cover up who you really are inside."

"It's very lonely, feeling like an outcast. Like you are invited to a costume party, but you are the only one in a mask."

"Do you have a lot of vampire friends in Romania? I bet you miss them."

"My dad procures art for his galleries in several countries. So we traveled quite a bit. By the time I made a friend, it was time to leave."

"What about humans, like me?" I asked, curling up next to him.

"There is no one like you, vampire or not," he said with a warm smile. "It's hard making human friends when you don't attend school, and it's even harder keeping them when they're eating their evening dinner and you are just rolling out of bed."

"Are your parents upset that you have a human girl-friend?"

"No. If they met you, they would immediately fall in love with you, just like I did," he said, and stroked my hair.

"I'd love to travel and live in the nighttime and sleep during the day. Your world seems so romantic. Being bonded to one another for an eternity. Flying off into the night together. Thirsting for no one but each other."

"I feel that way about your world."

"The grass is always greener, I guess. Or, in our case, blacker."

"When I'm with you," he began, "I don't care which world we are in, just as long as we're in the same one together."

"**W**ake up," Alexander gently whispered in my ear.

I opened my eyes to find that I had crashed out on the couch in his TV room as he stroked my hair. *Kissing Coffins* was playing on his oversized flat screen.

Jenny had desperately entered Professor Livingston's office at the university.

"I knew I'd find you here!" she exclaimed, finding Vladimir seated at his desk, his head buried in a textbook.

"You weren't supposed to come," he warned, without looking up, "to my house or to my study. You have put yourself in danger."

In the distance, there was an eerie howling.

"Why did you let me fall asleep?" I asked Alexander, lifting my head from his shoulder. "Did you put a spell on me?"

"You suggested we watch this," he replied. "But you conked out as soon as I pressed 'Play.' Besides, it's late and you've been through a lot."

"Late?" I asked, stretching my arms. "For you it's the middle of the day."

Jenny looked toward the window. "They are coming for me," she confessed to Vladimir nervously. "They want me to be one of . . . you."

Vladimir methodically turned the page of his book. He didn't look up. Another eerie howling was heard in the distance.

"I'll walk you home," Alexander offered as we rose to our feet. He kindly handed me his black leather jacket.

"But I want to stay here," I whined.

"You can't. Your parents will be worried."

"I'll tell them I'm babysitting."

"For a seventeen-year-old?"

He put the coat around my shoulders.

"I had better go—" Jenny started, looking out the window of the study into the fog-layered darkness. "It was foolish of me to come."

"You'll be all alone here in this huge mansion," I said to Alexander, as I adjusted my wrinkled dress.

"I'm safe. Besides, I've sent for Jameson."

"As slow as he drives? It'll take him years to get here. I'll stay until he arrives," I said, sitting back down.

"Wait!" Vladimir called, his head still focused on his book.

Jenny stopped at the door. The professor rose and slowly walked to her. "Since I've met you, I haven't been myself," Vladimir confessed.

The howling continued.

"Come on, girl," Alexander said, nudging me.

"I was afraid I'd never see you again," Jenny said. "If I leave here without you, I may not be able to find you next time."

I stared at Jenny as if she had just proclaimed my own fear.

"But what if I never see you again?" I asked Alexander, pulling him close.

"Is tomorrow after sunset soon enough?"

"I can't leave," I told Alexander. "I thought I'd see you after the Welcome to the Neighborhood party. And the next night you were gone."

"I left to protect you, not to hurt you," he answered in a serious tone, sitting down next to me.

"Protect me from what?"

"From Jagger. From me. From my world."

"But you don't have to protect me."

"My world is not just filled with romance, like you think it is. There is danger."

"There can be risk anywhere. It's not exclusive to vampires. You just have to be careful."

"But I don't want you to be near danger in any world."

"I won't if we are together," I argued.

"I don't want you to think you have to change who you are to be with me," he said earnestly.

"I know that," I assured him.

"Or ask that you change."

"That's why you left Dullsville," I realized out loud. "You were afraid I'd want to become a vampire."

"Yes. But there was a more imminent danger presiding. A vampire with white hair."

"Jagger."

He nodded.

"Then why did you go to Hipsterville?"

"Hipsterville?" he asked, confused.

"That's what I call it," I confessed with a grin.

"Of course," he said with a laugh. "I got word from my parents that Jagger had found an apartment in 'Hipsterville' and was searching cemeteries in neighboring communities for my grandmother's monument. Once he'd found it, he would know which town I was living in."

"That was what the note meant," I remembered. "A warning that Jagger was on his way to find you. To seek revenge."

"What note?" he asked, confused.

"In your room," I confessed.

"You snuck into the Mansion after I left?"

I flashed him a cheesy grin.

"I should have known," he said, and smiled back. Then his playful tone turned serious. "But more important than finding me, he may have found you."

"Well, he did, but that was my own fault."

"I was going to head him off at the pass before he came to Dullsville—confront him before he confronted me. Jameson and I found an abandoned manor house so we could hide while I made my plan. But I didn't plan on one thing."

"I'd follow you?"

"I saw the most beautiful girl climbing down the backyard tree."

"That was you in the attic window?"

"Yes."

"So why didn't you—"

"I kept a close eye on you. I had to, didn't I?"

"So why is Jagger out to get you?"

A sharp howl came from the screen, distracting Alexander from my question.

"We need to get you to the cemetery—to sacred ground," Vladimir warned. The handsome professor led her through the dark, marshy woods, riddled with fog. Vladimir held Jenny close as the howling sounds grew louder.

Alexander and I were fixed on the movie.

"How can we be together," Jenny asked, "if I'm not a vampire?"

Suddenly the TV screen went black. Alexander placed the remote he was holding on the coffee table.

He stood up and held his hand out for me.

"How *can* we be together?" I asked, rising.

"How can we *not* be?" he reassured me. Alexander grabbed my hand, and I reluctantly followed him out of the Mansion and toward my house. I felt like a kid at Disney World at closing time.

The night air in Dullsville felt fresher than ever, the dark sky clearer, the wet grass crisper. "So why was Jagger seeking revenge?" I asked.

"It's a long story," he said, with a yawn.

Alexander seemed so content forgetting the past, our hands entwined as we walked side by side. But I wouldn't rest until I knew.

"I have all night. And you have 'til sunrise."

"You're right," he said, as we walked down the street.

"It was about a promise I never made."

"A promise?" I asked.

"To take a girl for all of eternity."

"What girl?"

"Jagger's twin sister, Luna."

"He has a twin?"

Alexander nodded.

"Well, who made the promise?" I questioned aloud.

"My family did the year the three of us were born."

"Like an arranged marriage?"

"It's more than marriage."

"So why Luna?"

"When she was born, it was said she didn't respond to the darkness but seemed to flourish in the light. She refused to drink anything besides milk. Desperate, her family took her to a local underground doctor who pronounced her 'human.'"

I laughed. Alexander didn't seem to find it funny.

"It just sounds strange to me, that's all," I said, as we turned a corner.

"Well, it wasn't funny to the Maxwells. They were devastated. Luna had to live her life in daylight, while her family lived at night. She never even bonded with Jagger. At that time of the agreement, my family and his were very close. It was understood that when Luna was eighteen, we'd meet for a covenant ceremony and unite together for eternity, ensuring her a place in the vampire world."

"So what happened?" I asked, as we cut across the lawn through Oakley Woods.

"As I grew up, my family traveled and our families

became distant. Because Luna and I lived in different worlds, I never even knew her. When it came time for the ceremony, I had seen her only a few times. She didn't know me, and she was going to be with me forever?"

"Well, you are quite handsome," I said coyly. "So what did you do?"

"When it came time to kiss her for eternity, I leaned over and kissed her good-bye."

"That must have been hard for you, being a vampire and all," I whispered.

"I was doing it for both of us. Of course, the Maxwells didn't see it that way. They felt that I had spurned Luna, therefore offending her entire family. They were outraged. My parents quickly arranged for me to come here with Jameson and live in my grandmother's Mansion."

"Wow. It really had to have been tough following your heart when it went against your vampire community," I said. "And even more difficult to have been forced to leave Romania because of that decision."

"When I saw this raven-haired beauty trick-or-treating from my attic window, I knew I'd rather spend an eternity alone waiting to see her again than spend one with someone I didn't love."

Just then we reached my front door. Alexander gave me a long good-night kiss.

"Tomorrow after sunset," I reminded him.

"And not a second later," he said.

Alexander waved to me as I opened the front door. I walked inside and turned around to wave good-bye.

He had already disappeared, just as I knew he would.

14

Changeling

"It's after midnight," my dad warned as I tiptoed past him watching ESPN in the family room.

"Dad, I'm sixteen. It's a weekend."

"But this is—" he began in a stern voice.

"I know, your house. And I'm your daughter, and until I'm on my own I'll live by your rules."

"Well, at least you were paying attention."

"You've been saying it to me since I was two."

"You've been sneaking out since you could walk."

"I'm sorry, it won't happen again," I said.

I handed him his soda that was sitting on the coffee table and gave him a good-night hug.

"I'm glad you had a good time at Aunt Libby's," he said. "But I'm also glad you're back home."

"Me, too, Dad. Me, too."

Exhausted, I crawled into bed without even removing my rain-dampened clothes. I switched off the *Edward*

Scissorhands light on my nightstand and licked my lips. Alexander's kisses still lingered on my mouth. I curled up with my Mickey Malice plush, wishing I were holding Alexander instead. As I lay in bed, I tossed and turned. I couldn't wait for tomorrow's sunset.

Moments later, I felt a presence stirring in the quiet. I glanced around, but all the shadows were from the furniture. I checked under my bed; even a bat couldn't squeeze between all the junk I had stashed underneath it. I opened my closet door, but the only clothes I found were on hangers or strewn on the floor. I tiptoed to my window and pulled back the curtain, looking out into our backyard.

"Alexander?"

I saw a darkened figure walking away from the house, into the night.

"Good night, my love," I said, pressing my hand to the window.

I returned to bed and fell asleep.

The next morning, I awoke with a jolt. Yesterday's events seemed like a dream.

When I rose in my stiffened clothes, I realized that those events were real.

"Why are you still in your outfit from yesterday?" my mom nagged when I entered the kitchen. "Don't they talk about proper hygiene in health class?"

I wiped my haggard eyes and stumbled to the bathroom. I peeled off my day-old clothes and stepped into the shower.

Warm water flowed over my pale skin. My black nail

and toe polish looked stark against the clear white tub and tile that surrounded me.

I was back in Dullsville and Alexander was in his Mansion. We could finally live our lives together. But my boyfriend was a vampire and his nemesis had come to hunt him down. I'd never thought Dullsville could be so, well, not dull!

My whole life had changed in just a few days. For sixteen years I'd been living the same monotonous existence. My greatest concern had been finding black nail polish in a pastel town. Now it was getting through a sun-filled day alone while Alexander slept peacefully in his Mansion. We wouldn't be able to go for afternoon bike rides, meet after school, or spend our weekend days hanging out.

It was hard to imagine that I wouldn't ever be able to share sunlight with him. I was beginning to have doubts that I could handle this new world.

"It was a blast! I bought you this," I said, and handed Becky a package as we sat on the Evans Park swings.

She opened a Hello Kitty journal. "Cool. Thanks!"

"They have the best stores ever! And I went to a place called the Coffin Club. I met this weird guy."

"Really? Matt and I just went to the movies."

"If I tell you a secret, a super-duper colossal secret, do you promise not to tell anyone?"

"Can I tell Matt?" she asked eagerly.

Matt, Matt, Matt—who cared about Matt when I was bursting to tell her about my encounter with Jagger and the truth about Alexander.

"Why are we talking about Matt when I have the biggest news of a lifetime?"

"Well, you always talk about Alexander," she barked back. Her porcelain cheeks flushed ruby red. "And I listen to you all the time. Just 'cause you went away and had exciting things happen doesn't mean I didn't, too."

I was surprised by Becky's outburst. It had been only a few days since she had hooked up with Matt, but if she felt for him half of what I felt for Alexander, I'd have to understand her intensity. Becky had always been so mousy. Now that she had her own beau, she had become more confident. Our relationship had changed. We had never had anyone before but each other.

"Fine," I said, reluctantly. "You're right. I'm glad you are going out with Matt. Someone as awesome as you should have an awesome boyfriend."

"Thanks, Raven. Now, what were you going to tell me?"

I paused, debating if she could handle the vampirey info.

"Is Matt going to show up here again?"

She nodded. "He's right behind you."

I guess I had my answer.

"So, Monster Girl, how's Monster Boy?" a male voice called as I left the park. I glanced around to find Trevor in his red-and-white soccer uniform.

"I thought I was done with you. Are you always going

to be in my face?" I asked.

"As long as you wear black I will be. Have you two made any Monster Babies yet?" he asked.

"No, but when we do, I'll be sure to name one after you."

I walked away, and Trevor continued to follow.

"How do you do it? Play soccer, spend your daddy's money, and annoy people, all at the same time?" I asked.

"I could do more than annoy you, if you'd let me," he said, coyly fixing his green eyes on me.

"So that line isn't working on the cheerleaders anymore?"

If Trevor had ever truly bothered me before, he was now just a pest given what I'd recently been through.

"I still think there's something fishy going on in that mansion," he said, unrelenting.

"Give it a rest."

"Don't you think it's strange that Alexander's never seen during the day?"

"I wish *you* weren't seen during the day. Besides, he's homeschooled."

"My mom told me she spotted that freaky butler man hanging out at the butcher."

"Yeah. That is strange. The butler eats food. Who knew?"

"He requested 'the freshest, bloodiest meat you have.'"

"Would you prefer they drink your blood?" I teased.

He looked at me in shock.

"Get a life," I said. "Maybe your mom should be

paying attention to you more and gossiping less."

"You leave my mother—"

"I really don't have time for you or your mother anymore. Maybe it's time you get a new best friend," I said, and walked away.

15

Nightmare

I mpatient, I arrived at the Mansion before sunset. Jameson's Mercedes was once again parked in the driveway.

I sat on the uneven front steps, picking at the dandelions and weeds growing between the cracking cement. The door slowly creaked open.

Jameson greeted me.

"I'm so glad you're back," I said, squeezing his bony frame.

"I am, too, Miss Raven. I missed the Mansion and our favorite guest."

"I missed you, too. And I know one fabulous lady who was bummed that you were gone. . . ."

"Miss Ruby?" he asked, his eyes coming alive.

"Are you going to call her?" I asked.

"After what I've done? I couldn't."

"You have to! Besides, it wasn't your fault. Just tell her

you were unexpectedly called out of town."

"She'd never forgive me. And she shouldn't."

"Ruby loved the flowers. Besides, there's a carnival this weekend. She'll need a date. And you'll need one, too."

I could see Jameson pondering the decision, excited about seeing Ruby again, but unsure if he could muster the courage to call her.

Alexander bounced down the grand staircase, wearing black jeans and a black HIM T-shirt. He gave me a long hello kiss.

"That was sweet of you to come by last night," I said, in his arms.

"I didn't come by," he said, confused.

"You didn't? I saw a guy in my backyard."

Alexander looked worried.

"I bet it was Trevor," I guessed. "I saw him after school. I think he still blames me for his plummeting popularity."

"If you need me to talk to him, I will."

I'd always defended myself from Trevor. It was refreshing to finally have someone who would stand up for me. "You are my superhero!" I exclaimed, and gave him a hug.

"I found this really cool place."

"Cool place? In Dullsville?"

He grabbed my hand and led me out of the Mansion and down the street.

"It's so ironic that the rumors Trevor started turned out to be true," I said to my vampire boyfriend.

"About me, or you?" he teased.

"I mean, I thought you were . . . then I didn't. But then I did. And then when I totally didn't again, I found out you were."

"Now I'm confused. Am I? Or am I not?"

"That is the question." I squeezed his hand.

"I just don't want to lose you or put you in danger."

"I love danger."

When we passed Dullsville's cemetery, I wondered where we were going.

"Just a little bit farther," he assured me.

I would walk to China if Alexander were by my side. I had so many questions burning inside me, I didn't know which to ask first.

"Did you grow up with Jagger?"

"Our families were close when we were born. I think he was jealous of Luna. With her living as a human, he knew what he was missing—school, sports, friends. He is scrawny, but I think he really dreamed of being a jock like Trevor. I kind of feel sorry for him. He wasn't able to find something he enjoyed, besides revenge. But then my family traveled. My parents were bohemians, and we really never fit in with our kind. We were what was known as vampire vegetarians."

"Cool. So how do you survive? Connections with the butcher?" I joked, referring to my conversation with Trevor.

"How did you know?" he asked, surprised. "We also have family who have ties to blood banks."

"Uh . . . I just guessed," I replied. "My parents were hippies, too. They wouldn't eat anything with eyeballs. But they traded their hippie threads and beaded satchels for Armani suits and briefcases, and they drive their BMWs past PETA protesters on their way to work."

"Sounds like our parents would make great friends."

"Just like us."

Alexander squeezed my hand.

"I sometimes wonder what it would be like if you changed me. We could stay up all night long, fly into the night, and be bonded for eternity."

"I've imagined what it would be like if I were born like you. We could go to the same school, lie out in the sun, have picnics in the park. I'd be able to see us reflected together in a mirror. I'd fill my walls with pictures of us at the beach."

"We share similar dreams."

"You're a human who wants to be a vampire, and I'm a vampire who wants to be human."

I gazed up at Alexander with empathy. I hadn't realized he felt as alone in his own world as I did in mine.

"It's just over there," he said, pointing to an abandoned barn across the train tracks.

The red barn had seen better days. Boards from the gray roof and side were missing, like teeth on a smiling kindergartner.

We stepped through the door frame. The door was missing, but the wooden beams that held the barn together still remained intact. Vacant stalls stood on one side, an empty hayloft on the other. Alexander grabbed a gas lantern that hung from a hook on the wall and turned it on. He took my hand and led me toward a darkened corner.

"Are we going up into the hayloft?" I asked coyly.

"Follow me," he said. "Don't be afraid. They won't bite," he said with a laugh.

"Who's they?" I wondered. I imagined a family of vampires, hiding out in the stable. Maybe long-lost relatives of his.

I held his hand hard as he pulled me into the corner of the abandoned barn. I could see two slanted eyes staring back at me from the corner. I stepped into the moonlight to discover a powder white mama cat with a litter of snowball white baby kittens—and there in the mix by herself was one teeny black cat.

"She's just like me!" I exclaimed.

"I thought you'd like her."

"She's the cutest thing I've ever seen! I want her to come home with me," I said wishfully, kneeling down and staring at the kitten.

"I found them last night."

"You want me to keep her?"

"She's finished nursing. And the mother can't care for them all."

Alexander and I sat off to the side and watched as the kittens purred and the mama fell asleep.

"I'm surprised she isn't hissing at us," I said.

"She understands we're not here to hurt her, but to help her."

"So, you're like Dr. Dolittle with a bite."

He grimaced at my joke. "Do you want the cat or not?"

I nodded my head eagerly.

Alexander picked up the tiny black kitten, who looked like a small ball of yarn in his handsome hands.

"It's okay," he said, handing her to me.

I held the tiniest black baby kitten I'd ever seen. She licked her mouth and looked up at me as if she were smiling.

"I can keep her?"

"I wanted you to have something to remember me by."

"Remember you?"

"To keep you company during the day."

"That is the sweetest thing!"

I stared down at my Gothic Gift gazing up at me with teeny lime green eyes.

"I'll call her Nightmare."

16

Vampire Visitor

"Where did you get that?" Billy Boy asked when I brought Nightmare into the house.

"Alexander gave her to me."

"She's so cute. But you'll have to hide her from Dad. You know how he feels about pets."

"I know, but I'm not bringing a lizard home this time. It's just a kitty."

"Where'd you get that?" my dad asked, coming down the stairs.

"Alexander gave her to me."

"I don't care if the president gave it to you. It has to go."

"Paul, she is really cute," my mom commented, petting Nightmare's head. "And Raven is certainly old enough to be responsible for a cat."

"Her age is not what I'm concerned about," he warned.

"Dad, didn't I prove enough to you by working at Armstrong Travel? I'm not a little girl anymore."

He paused as I held my Nightmare up to his face.

"Fine. But she stays in your room. I don't want her running all around the kitchen countertops or scratching on my couch."

"Thanks, Dad." I gave him a huge hug and kiss on his cheek.

"Now I'll show you your new home," I said to Nightmare as I took her to my bedroom.

I looked around my room. I didn't know where to put her.

"I have an old box in the garage filled with clothes from college that would be a perfect bed for her," Mom said, peeking in. "It's above the tools. Bring me the box and I'll repack the clothes."

"Thanks."

I started to close my bedroom door when Nightmare began to follow me.

"I'll be right back, sweetie," I said, putting her in the middle of the floor. "I'm going to make you a bed."

Nightmare's ears perked up, and she looked at the window. She darted up onto my computer chair and then onto my desk. She stared out the window, hissing. I picked her up and placed her on my bed.

"I'll be right back. Sleep here for now."

When I reached my bedroom door, Nightmare was back at my feet, her lime green eyes squinting at me. She hissed at me and pawed at my boots.

I picked her up. "Mommy will be right back." I kissed my new kitty on the nose, placed her back on the floor, and quickly closed the door. I could hear her scratching against the wood as I ran down the hall.

I walked to our garage at the end of our driveway. I stood on my dad's toolbox as I searched for the box. I could hear the crickets.

There was a lot of rustling in the tree by my bedroom window. I froze.

More rustling. It could be a squirrel. Or having just seen Trevor last night, I thought he could be toilet papering my window.

I turned off the garage light and tiptoed over to the tree. But now the leaves were still. Not a bird. Not a squirrel. Not a soccer snob.

I headed back to the garage, and then I saw Jagger.

I gasped.

"What are you doing here?"

"I just wanted to see you."

"I thought you went back to Romania," I said, stepping back.

"I was hoping you would come with me."

"Alexander assured me that the feud was over and you were gone for good."

"That is why you can't tell him," he said. "Otherwise, not only will your safety and Sterling's be in jeopardy, but the whole town's."

"The whole town?" I asked.

"Don't tempt me," he said, licking his lips. "You

wouldn't like to know what happens when a small town finds out a vampire is living among them and dating one of their daughters."

I froze. I remembered how easily Dullsville was sucked into Trevor's rumor, resulting in gossip and graffiti. If the town had proof of Alexander's true identity, there was no predicting what people would do.

"Fine, I won't tell him. But you must leave now!"

Jagger only stepped closer.

"I'm not going back to the cemetery with you," I argued, backing up. "I'll scream if I have to. My father is inside and he's a lawyer."

"That won't be necessary. Why spend your life sitting in a mansion with a sensitive artist watching paint dry when we could see the world together?"

"I'm not going anywhere with you!"

"Well, I'm sure you could persuade me to stay in town. In fact, I'm beginning to like it here."

"I don't want you! Your feud is over with Alexander. Go home already—"

"Feud? I have other things on my mind now. Alexander might be able to deny who he is, but I can't deny who I am."

His blue and green eyes shot through me. I looked away, afraid he'd make me dizzy again. He began to lean into me.

"Raven!" Billy Boy called from the back door.

My brother ran down the steps holding Nightmare. Jagger stepped back into the shadows.

"Billy Boy! Go inside. Now!" I exclaimed, running toward him.

"What's taking you so long?" Billy Boy asked. "Nightmare is throwing a freak attack. I found her pawing against your bedroom door."

I blocked Billy Boy's step. Frantically, I turned around, shielding him.

The backyard was empty. Jagger was gone.

I pulled Billy Boy inside and locked the door.

"I've never been so happy to see you!" I said, squeezing my little brother, Nightmare in his hands.

"What's wrong with you?" he asked, cringing like I had cooties.

"I just thought I saw the bogeyman."

"You watch too many scary movies," he said.

"I sometimes feel like I'm starring in them," I replied.

As much as I hated going back to school after spring break, I knew at least my daylight hours brought a safe reprieve from Jagger.

I returned to Dullsville High a different person than when I had left—as if being the only goth in a conservative town hadn't made me different enough. I couldn't concentrate in class, knowing I was privy to a secret world of vampires.

Classmates continued to bury their heads in textbooks and anticipate the next soccer game, while I doodled in my journal and couldn't wait for the next sunset.

I was still an outcast, but I think my classmates got a rise that Trevor had been dethroned from his kingdom. And although they didn't high-five me in the hallway or invite me to their parties, I was actually given a cutter's privilege at the drinking fountain.

"It's a shame Alexander is homeschooled. It would be nice to eat lunch as a foursome," Becky said at lunch on the baseball bleachers.

"Yeah, that would rock."

"But still, we should do something together."

"How about going to the drive-in?" Matt asked, as he walked up the bleachers behind me. "*Kissing Coffins* is playing tonight. Admission is half price if you wear a costume."

"Cool! I've always wanted to see it on the big screen. I'm sure Alexander would love to go."

"And I'll be able to see what happens to Jenny," Becky said excitedly. "I can dress as one of the town's vampires and wear a cape."

"And fangs!" I added.

Just then Trevor walked onto the field with his soccer-snob groupies. He looked up at Matt, who sat down next to Becky.

As much as Trevor tormented me and as pathetic as I thought he was, I felt a tinge of pity for him. He was an even sadder case now that he was Matt-less. I watched Matt offer Becky his sandwich.

"I'm glad you got traded to our team," I said to Matt, who closed his brown bag and gave me a warm smile.

After school, Becky and I searched through my closet to find her a costume to wear to the drive-in.

"Man, you do have a lot of black," she said, as I tossed out dozens of skirts and shirts for her to choose from.

Becky modeled black tights, a black miniskirt, and a lacy black chemise.

"That's perfect. You'll be one of the members of the vampire gang who tries to convert Jenny. I just need my outfit."

I heard my mom's SUV pull into the driveway, and Becky and I raced to meet her at the back door.

"Can I have an advance on my allowance?" I asked hurriedly.

"Calm down," she advised. "Don't I even get a hello?"

"Hello," I replied. "Now, can I have an advance on my allowance?"

"I hope you didn't bid on a Hello Batty toaster on eBay again. I thought we told you—"

"I want to dye my hair blond."

"Blond?" she asked, shocked. "You are not going to ruin your gorgeous black hair."

"But it needs to be blond to complete my costume."

"Are you in a play?"

"Well, sort of."

"For school?"

"No, I just need your help."

"Well, I have some wigs from college in the box I emptied for Nightmare. I know there's an auburn one. There may be a blond one, too."

"Can we go see?" I begged.

Mom reluctantly put her purse down on the kitchen table, and Becky and I followed her into my parents' bedroom.

She rummaged through an old Harrod's shopping bag. "Here it is!" she exclaimed, as if she'd found a sunken treasure. She handed me a weathered blond wig. "I wore this in college. Your father loved it!"

I rolled my eyes. "I also need a white dress," I confessed.

She looked at me, pleased, as if her rebellious daughter were finally asking to borrow pearls. "I'll see what I have!" she replied gleefully.

She picked up a pair of flared denims with rhinestones from the box. "Do you believe I once wore these?" she asked, holding them against her pleated Ann Taylor skirt.

"I have a white blouse," she said.

"Ahh. Here's a white eyelet skirt."

"Perfect."

My mom stuck the wig on my head, and I held the clothes in front of me.

"It's like looking at a teenage version of myself," she said fondly.

I threw the skirt and blouse in the wash, and Becky and I returned to my room.

"We are so going to rock!" I said. "But we just need one thing to complete our outfits."

I hunted through my dresser drawers, closet shelves, and boxes underneath my bed.

Halloween was months ago, and in a town like Dullsville it was easier to find a fake Prada purse than fake teeth.

Frustrated, I banged on Billy Boy's door. He opened it

slightly, sticking his Charlie Brown–shaped head out. I could barely see Henry typing at my brother's computer.

"Did you take my vampire teeth?" I accused him.

"Why would I want your nasty saliva near me?" Billy Boy said, starting to close the door on me.

"Well, I can't find them, and I have to have them for tonight," I argued, pressing the door back open.

Henry rushed over to the door. "I have some," he offered. "Never been used."

Henry and Billy Boy rode their bikes, and I followed with Becky on mine. We must have been quite a sight as we headed to Henry's house at the edge of Oakley Woods— two goths and two nerds riding alongside one another.

We parked our bikes in Henry's driveway and entered the colonial-style five-bedroom house.

We were greeted by his housekeeper, who was folding laundry.

We walked up the pristine wooden stairs to his bedroom. A NO YUPPIES ALLOWED sign hung on his door.

"I like that," I said.

A spongy black doormat rested on the floor, and a million dead bolts sealed his door.

"What are you hiding inside? Secret recipes of cafeteria food?" I asked.

After he unlocked the outside dead bolts, he stepped onto the mat. His bedroom door sprung open automatically.

Henry had a loft bed, with a metallic blue computer

underneath. Stars were pasted on his ceiling, I'm sure in astronomically correct order. A solar system mobile hung from his ceiling fan. A telescope stood by his window.

He slid open his walk-in closet doors to reveal neatly stacked, clear plastic shoe boxes.

"Five dollars gets you samples," he said, pointing to them.

Each box was labeled: ACNE. BLOOD. PIMPLES. PUKE. SCARS.

"Who wants to have more pimples?" I asked.

"And I have smells. Here," he said, opening a beaker and pushing it under my nose.

"Gross!" I said, repulsed. "It smells like the bathroom after Billy Boy uses it."

"Shut up!" my brother said.

"I like to pour this on Mrs. Louis's chair sometimes," he said proudly. "Look around. I have them alphabetized."

"I should have known."

Becky and I each handed over our money and loaded our pockets with ghoulish goodies.

When we were finished, Henry held a box before me as if he were holding the Holy Grail. He opened it, revealing two exact replicas of human teeth in the shape of fangs.

"With the glue, seven dollars."

I knew I had only six in my purse.

"Five dollars and a stick of gum," I offered.

"Six. And your school picture," he countered.

I looked hard at him, then at Becky.

"But you inscribed it to me!" she said.

"Please," I begged, flashing her my puppy-dog eyes.

She opened her wallet and handed Henry the picture.

I handed him the money and left before he changed his mind.

As I headed out to meet Alexander for our date, I found my parents in the kitchen, paying bills.

"I'm going to be out a teensy bit late tonight," I advised.

"It's a school night," my mother said.

"I know, but we're going to the drive-in," I said with a smile.

"Why don't you wait until the weekend?" my mom asked.

"Because tonight's half price if you wear a costume. Becky and Matt are going, too."

"Becky?" my mother asked, surprised.

"Yes, my little Becky. It'll be our first double date. Besides, I already did my homework, and we have a sub for first bell anyway."

"Seems like you had all your excuses lined up," my father said.

"I'll take care of the dishes all week," I said to my mother. "And Dad, I'll wash your car."

"Last time you washed my car, you put Wicked Wiccas stickers on it."

"But you have to admit, it looked cool."

"And last time you took care of the dishes, you broke

Grandma's teapot," my mother remembered.

"Fine. Then we have a deal," I began. "I'll just go to the movie, and I'll save you trouble by not doing your chores."

"How did that just happen?" my dad wondered, as I headed for the front door. "And when you're finished with that blond wig, your mother needs it back."

I slung my backpack filled with my *Kissing Coffins* accessories on my shoulder and grabbed a container of garlic powder from the kitchen. I held it tightly in my hand, as if I were holding a can of Mace, as I walked to the Mansion. If Jagger jumped out at me, I wanted to be protected.

I felt a familiar lurking presence as I turned the corner to Benson Hill. I saw a rustling in a bush and blond strands poking through the branches. I took a deep breath, and I quietly opened the container of garlic powder and threw it hard, directly into the brush.

"Ouch!" a male's voice cried.

Trevor jumped out of the bush and held his forehead.

"What are you doing?" I shouted at him.

"I saw you coming up the road and wanted to scare you," he said, rubbing his wound.

"You don't have to hide. Your face alone could scare Frankenstein."

I grabbed the container from the sidewalk and replaced it in my purse.

I walked away, and Trevor continued to follow me as we drew closer to the gate.

"I really don't have time for you anymore," I said. "I'm going to the drive-in." And I slipped past the slightly open iron gate.

"You have a pretty good arm. You should try out for the baseball team. And tell your gothic boyfriend," he called, "if he wants to apply, they could use a batboy."

I left Trevor and was walking up the Mansion's driveway when I overheard him talking to someone outside the gate. I glanced back and saw my nemesis from behind, standing next to a guy with white hair.

I stopped. Jagger and Trevor? A dangerous duo.

I sneaked back down the driveway and hid behind a bush next to the wrought-iron gate.

"Hey, watch out, dude!" Trevor hollered. He must have bumped into Jagger in the darkness.

I could only imagine Trevor's reaction to the shock of seeing the pale, tattooed, multipierced Jagger walking alone on a darkened street. I wasn't sure if Trevor would hit him or take off running.

"Sorry," Jagger said in a cool voice. "I didn't see you coming.

"It's so dark around here," Jagger continued, shifting his feet.

"Yeah, I think the Sterlings knock out the streetlamps on purpose."

Jagger laughed. "That babe you were walking with. She's your girlfriend?" he asked.

"Raven? She's my nightmare. No, she hangs out with

the dude who lives in the Mansion. I've never seen you around here before," he said, scrutinizing him.

"I'm just visiting. I'm Sterling's friend."

"Friend? I didn't think he had any," he said with a laugh. "Well, you better catch him before they go to the drive-in."

"The drive-in?" Jagger asked.

"Yeah. It's built on an ancient burial ground," he whispered, as if revealing a secret. "I've heard that late at night, you can see ghosts eating popcorn."

"Burial ground?" Jagger wondered aloud. "Perfect."

"For what?" Trevor asked, confused.

"Uh . . . a club initiation," Jagger rambled. "But it's a very exclusive club. . . . Maybe in the future you could join."

"Thanks anyway. Soccer takes all my free time. Besides, Sterling doesn't seem like the type to belong to a club."

"He's already a member. I just have to persuade Raven to join. Maybe I'll surprise them there," Jagger said. "Can you point me in the right direction?"

"Follow me," Jagger's new ally said. "It's on the way to the game."

As the two left together, my mouth hung open in disbelief.

Jagger was planning to have a covenant ceremony tonight at the drive-in, with me as his covenant girl!

I needed a plan fast.

I took a deep breath and tried to think. If I canceled our double date, Jagger could return to my house, putting not only me but my family in danger.

I didn't have much time to find a way to keep Jagger away for good without ending up as his dinner. Why couldn't Alexander and I just enjoy a movie together? Like *Kissing Coffins*, which reflected my own imminent situation—a movie about the vampire Vladimir Livingston, who tried to save the innocent mortal ingénue Jenny from the depths of the darkened Underworld.

And then it hit me.

Jagger was planning to take me tonight at the drive-in? But he couldn't. Not if I was already taken by someone else first.

Kissing Coffins

"It's hard, you know, without a mirror," I commented anxiously in Alexander's room as I awkwardly tried to glue my fake fangs onto my teeth. The soundtrack to *Kissing Coffins* was blaring in the background. "Are they straight?" I flashed him a sexy vampire smile.

"Wow!" he said, impressed. "Are you sure they are plastic?" He touched them with his fingers. "They look so real."

"Be careful. They aren't dry," I snapped.

"Why are you so nervous? It's just a movie."

"But it's not. I have something to tell you. Promise you won't be mad at me."

"Okay. Does it involve another guy?"

"Yes, but not in the way you think. Jagger's still in Dullsville."

"How do you know?" he asked, shocked.

"I just saw him," I confessed.

"Where?"

"Outside the Mansion with Trevor."

"Trevor? That's the last person he should be talking to."

"Well, I saw Jagger the other night, too, at my house. But he warned me that if I told you, he would tell everyone about you."

"He was at your house?" he asked angrily. "Did he hurt you?"

"No," I assured him. "But he plans to, tonight, at the drive-in. Trevor told Jagger it was built on sacred ground and Jagger persuaded Trevor to show him where it was. Before, Jagger wanted me just to get even with you. Now I just think he wants me for himself—unless he is convinced that I have already been taken."

"But—"

"I'll need you to convince him."

"But that means—"

"Just like Vladimir saves Jenny in the movie. It will be so romantic."

"I don't know if I can."

"You have to. We have no other choice."

I gave him a reassuring kiss. "It will be okay. Trust me."

I fluffed my hair. I spun around and modeled my outfit. "How do I look?"

"I like you as a blond," he said, half distracted.

"And you look like Vladimir," I complimented him, as I smoothed his dark suit and straightened his black cape.

"You look just like Jenny," he said.

"But I want to see for myself."

I grabbed my purse off his bed, opened it, and reached inside, searching for Ruby's compact.

Alexander pulled at his stomach. "I don't feel so well."

"You're just nervous. I promise you, it will be okay."

"I really don't—"

"Wait a minute," I said, scrounging for a peppermint.

"What's that?" he asked, repulsed when I offered it to him.

"It's just a mint," I answered. "Don't they have them in Romania? It settles your stomach."

"Get it away from me," he said, refusing the mint and stepping away.

Then I smelled something odd coming from inside my purse.

I stuck my hand inside, and buried underneath my wallet and a huge wad of tissues was the cause.

"Oh no! It's my garlic powder," I said, holding the plastic container toward him. The lid had opened.

"Put that away!" he said, holding his stomach.

"I'm sorry!" I said, fumbling and stepping away from him.

"Farther. Like in Utah!"

"I didn't mean to—" I apologized.

His ghost-white face grew even more gaunt with every breath he took.

I opened the attic window and threw the plastic container as hard as I could, far into the night sky.

Alexander was still stepping back from me, his breathing getting heavier.

"I'll throw my purse out, if I have to."

But he said nothing as he gasped for air.

"Jameson!" I called, but the *Kissing Coffins* soundtrack was playing too loudly for anyone to hear.

I ran out of the bedroom and down the attic steps. "Jameson!" I cried. "Jameson!" I didn't hear a sound as I barreled through the second floor. I flew down the grand staircase. Why did he have to live in such a big house?

I burst through the kitchen door and found Jameson putting dishes into the dishwasher.

"Alexander!" I gasped. "He was exposed to garlic! Call nine-one-one!"

Jameson's eyes grew even buggier than usual, making me even more terrified of the tragic state of the situation. But then he collected himself and opened a cabinet door.

Lying on the shelf was an antidote. Jameson handed me the shot.

"You must give it to him in his leg," he ordered.

"I must?" I said, shocked.

"By the time I climb those stairs, Miss Raven, it may be too late."

I grabbed the shot from his slender hand and ran.

My heart raced as I took off up the grand staircase, doubtful I would get to Alexander in time.

I rushed into the room to find Alexander lying on his back on his bed, his skin turning blue and his eyes growing vacant. His breath was shallow.

I remembered watching *Pulp Fiction*. A nervous John Travolta wound up his arm and slammed a shot into Uma Thurman's arrested heart. I wondered if I could be so brave.

I placed a shaking hand on Alexander's thigh and raised the shot. "One. Two. Three." I bit my lip and jammed the injection into his leg.

I waited. But Alexander didn't move. How long did it take? Was I too late?

"Alexander! Talk to me! Please!"

Suddenly, Alexander sat up, rigid, his eyes wide open. He breathed a full breath of air as if sucking in all the oxygen in the room.

Then he breathed out, and his body relaxed.

He looked up at me with weary eyes.

"Are you okay?" I asked. "I didn't mean to—"

"I need some—" he tried to say.

"Blood?" I asked, worried.

"No. Water."

Just then Jameson came into the room with a tall glass.

I held the glass to his lips. Alexander quickly drank it down. With every gulp his eyes grew more alive.

"Your face looks almost pale again," I said eagerly.

Jameson and I breathed a sigh of relief as Alexander recovered.

"Why were you carrying garlic?" Alexander finally asked.

"In case Jagger visited me again."

"Jagger?" Jameson asked, alarmed. "He's here?"

Alexander and I nodded.

"Then shouldn't we go? Is Miss Raven safe?"

I grabbed Alexander's hand. "Batman saved me from his evil nemesis before. And tonight he will for good."

The closest I'd been to Dullsville's drive-in was when Becky and I were in elementary school. We would sit outside the surrounding fence and watch a blockbuster movie in the crisp grass, eating popcorn and candy we brought from home. If we were lucky enough, the patrons would have their movie speakers turned on full blast. If not, Becky and I would provide our own dialogue and crack up until a security guard shooed us away.

Never in my wildest dreams did I imagine that Becky and I would be driving through the gates of Dullsville's drive-in with two boyfriends.

When the rumors about Dullsville's drive-in being built on an ancient burial ground began, it was forced to shut down. But the only thing excavators discovered buried in the dirt were worms, and the theater had recently reopened. The smell of fresh paint mixed with the night air. Metallic gray speakers hung on stands next to the arriving cars. A yellow-and-white snack bar and picnic tables sat fifty yards behind the last parked car.

As Alexander drove Matt, Becky, and me through the parking lot, couples were wearing homemade capes and slicked-back hair, while little kids sporting pajamas and bat wings hung out on hoods and roofs of cars. Schoolmates from Dullsville High wore black T-shirts and jeans. It was obvious that no one but Alexander and me had actually seen the film. Alexander and I were the only patrons who came dressed as Vladimir and Jenny; everyone only knew it was a vampire movie, so they just wore black. The moviegoers stared at us as we drove through the crowd.

We found a spot in the back of the drive-in, and the four of us got out of the car to decide on snacks.

I had other things on my mind besides popcorn. As the three of them discussed "to butter or not to butter," I tiptoed around the parking lot. Jagger could be anywhere, waiting to sink his fangs into my neck.

Alexander found me hunting around the bushes.

"Come here," he said, leading me back to the car. "He's spoiled enough of our fun. We should at least try to enjoy ourselves. Look around. Tonight, we're not outcasts," Alexander said, and gave me a squeeze. He was right. I glanced at the crowd, larger than Alexander's Welcome to the Neighborhood party.

"This is way cool," I said, for a moment forgetting about the impending danger.

Matt and Becky returned with popcorn and drinks. The previews started, and we got back into the car—Matt and Becky in the backseat and Alexander and me in the front.

I immediately locked the doors.

"What are you doing?" Matt asked. "It's a drive-in."

"Keeping out the riffraff," I said.

Just then a preteen boy with straws stuck on his teeth for fangs pressed his face against my window.

"See!" I said, as we all laughed. I leaned against the window, bugged my eyes, and flashed my vampire teeth.

The boy's mouth dropped open, and his straws fell to the ground. "Mom!" he cried, and ran off.

"That was awful," Becky admonished.

"But funny," Matt confirmed.

We munched on our snacks and cuddled as the previews ended and the movie began. All the while, Alexander and I anxiously glanced outside for any vampire activity.

"I don't think I can do this," Alexander whispered when he caught me focusing on the picnic tables instead of the movie screen.

"Of course you can." I could see the concern in his eyes. I leaned over and gave him a kiss on the mouth.

"Hey, we can't see," Matt and Becky said.

Alexander and I laughed, a great relief from the nervous tension that had been building up in us. I cuddled next to him and, for a while, forgot about Jagger. We got lost in the moment, and Alexander and I recited the lines of the movie together.

Three-quarters of the way through the film, at the moment that the vampire Vladimir was bringing Jenny to a graveyard wedding, the screen turned yellow, and the film burned and crumbled. We could hear a flapping sound.

The crowd began yelling "Boo!"

"Aw, man," I heard Matt say.

"It's all a conspiracy to make us buy more popcorn," I said.

We climbed out of the car and stretched.

"I could use a drink. You guys want anything?" Matt asked.

"Thanks anyway," I said.

"I'll go with you," Becky offered. Matt grabbed her hand, and they left for the snack bar.

"Should we be concerned about them?" I asked, feeling uneasy.

"Jagger wants you, not a soccer match."

I looked around. My heart started to race.

"Now I'm getting nervous," I said.

"Why don't you relax in the car. I'll stand guard."

I opened the driver's-side door, jumped in, and quickly locked the door.

I turned to lock the passenger door and gasped.

Jagger was sitting next to me!

"You thought I wouldn't recognize you with blond hair," he sneered.

I tried to open the door, but he grabbed my arm.

"I've come to collect what I didn't collect before," he said, looking into my eyes, his fangs primed. I pushed him away just as I heard a banging on my window. I looked up to see an enraged Alexander.

He tried to open my door as I struggled to keep Jagger's fangs at bay.

Frustrated, Alexander ran to the other side as Jagger automatically locked all the doors.

"Help!" I cried, pushing him at arm's length.

Alexander returned to my window, balling his fist to

punch through the glass, when I managed to wedge my feet in front of Jagger. I stretched one hand toward the window, my fingers reaching as far as they could, and barely touched the lock. With all my might, I managed to lift the knob with my index finger.

My door flung open, but Jagger pulled me out the passenger door before Alexander could reach me.

He dragged me away from the car and toward the back of the drive-in.

But before Jagger reached the exit, Alexander caught up and grabbed his arm. "Let her go!" he demanded, "before I—"

Jagger's grip remained tight around my wrist.

"I came to do what you could never do," Jagger said.

"What does he mean?" I asked.

Alexander flashed his fangs at Jagger and stepped in between us. "Don't make me do this in front of those people," Alexander said, referring to a few patrons in the distance who were looking at us curiously.

I backed away, out of reach of Jagger.

"This would never have happened," Jagger continued. "My sister just wanted to be like everyone else. She could have had anyone. But we chose you! And you left her standing all alone!"

"You know why. I never meant to hurt her or your family," Alexander defended.

"You'll do the same thing to Raven. You really were never like one of us. You may deny who you are," Jagger yelled, "but I won't deny who I am!"

He ran toward me and grabbed my arm just as Alexander grabbed the other.

Then Jagger flashed his fangs and lunged at my neck.

"It's too late!" I hollered, ducking away. "Alexander already has me." I leaned in and bit Jagger's arm.

Suddenly the parking lot lights dimmed and the movie started again. The vampire Vladimir was leading Jenny by the hand through the cemetery. A gang of vampires was following them, trying in vain to stop the ceremony and take the ingénue for their own.

Jagger howled out in pain as I pulled Alexander toward the movie screen.

Alexander resisted. "Where are you going? We can't turn our backs on him."

I gazed up at the screen. Vladimir was leading Jenny to the tombs. "We don't have much time."

But Alexander stared back at Jagger, whose pale face was turning red.

"Just like we planned. Please, trust me," I begged him, tugging his hand.

Alexander glanced over his shoulder. Jagger was heading straight for us.

I could see Becky and Matt coming through the parking lot with drinks in their hands.

"Hey, what's going on?" Becky asked as she got closer.

"I can't talk now, but get in the car and lock the doors!" I commanded.

Alexander and I hurried toward the front of the lot, where the movie screen was.

An angry Jagger lurked behind us.

"What is Raven doing?" I heard Becky ask, as she and Matt got into the Mercedes.

Alexander and I stood in front of the movie screen and our *Kissing Coffins* mirror images.

Patrons began hollering, "What's going on?"

I looked out into the crowd, but I couldn't see Jagger.

Then I noticed him hovering behind a family, only fifty feet away from us. When he caught my eye, he took off toward us.

"Hurry!" I exclaimed. "We don't have much time!"

As Vladimir lifted his beloved Jenny into his arms, I placed my arms around Alexander's neck. He lifted me up.

The crowd roared, clapping and tapping their horns as we acted out the movie behind us.

I could see out of the corner of my eye that Jagger was now only a few feet away, coming after me.

"Just like the film," I whispered.

Alexander anxiously looked into my eyes. My fist clenched by my side, primed for what was about to happen.

"Bite me, Alexander!" I cried. "Bite me!"

Jagger reached out. Alexander put his mouth on my neck just as the on-screen vampire did to his bride. I felt a slight pressure on my flesh. I grabbed my neck and cried out. My head slumped back, my body lay limp in his arms. My heart pulsed in overtime as if beating for both of us. I could feel the warm red liquid slowly dripping down my neck, the smell of blood permeating the air around us. Alexander lifted his head proudly, mirroring the on-screen vampire, holding his bride in his arms, a red river flowing from both vampires' lips.

The crowd cheered.

I glanced over to Jagger, whose blue and green eyes were now red with rage. Alexander gently let me down.

I was light-headed. I stumbled to my feet, holding my red-stained neck, as the liquid trickled down my forearm. As the camera moved to a close-up of Jenny's face, I looked at Jagger with a wicked grin and flashed my vampire fangs.

He began to howl with such a rage his body shook, but his cry was masked by the audience hollering and honking their car horns.

There was nothing left he could do to Alexander, nothing he could take.

Jagger's eyes grew redder, his muscles rippled, and he licked his fangs. He withdrew into the darkness and disappeared.

"I loved the way you acted out the movie last night!" Becky complimented me the next day at our lockers. "I had no idea you planned to do that. You totally rocked!"

"Thanks. I just had to wait for the right moment."

"Who would have known Vladimir would only pretend to bite Jenny so the vampires wouldn't covet her as one of their own."

"He does it so the vampires will believe Jenny has bonded eternally to him. They are forced to flee London and return to Romania, never to harm her again."

"Yeah, but you would think Vladimir would want to make her a vampire for himself."

"Well, the lesson is, not all vampires are bad," I said with a smile.

"They aren't?" Matt asked, standing behind us.

"Yes, just like soccer snobs," I teased.

"Well, I thought Alexander really bit you. Can I see your flesh wounds?" he added.

"Isn't that a personal question?" I kidded. "Besides, Alexander only pretended to bite me—just like Vladimir does to Jenny. He gave an award-winning performance," I said proudly. "I think he actually liked acting in front of all those people."

"Well, the blood looked real, too," he said.

"My brother's nerd-mate, Henry, has all these special effects. That's where I got these vampire teeth," I said, and flashed them.

"Why are you still wearing them?" he asked.

"I can't get them off. I think Henry charges extra for glue remover."

Just then two of Dullsville High's junior varsity cheerleaders stopped at our lockers.

"Like, can you tell me where I can get those costumes you wore last night?" one asked.

"You looked like Marilyn Monroe," the other cheerleader said to me. "And you looked like Elvira," she said to Becky. "I want a costume like Elvira."

Costume? I wondered. Hadn't they ever noticed I'd always dressed like that? I considered telling her about Hot Gothics in Hipsterville, or inviting her to come over to my house to borrow from my closet. But the thought of preppy cheerleaders dressing goth just because they thought it was "in" turned my stomach. I'd been an outcast for so long, I might have a hard time being an incast.

"You were awesome last night," her friend complimented. "Where did you get that blood?"

I was thinking of telling her about Henry, but decided to keep him my secret.

"It was real," I said.

"Ooh, gross!" they both exclaimed, and scurried away.

I had to admit, I liked the attention the drive-in performance brought me. Even if I knew it was going to last only as long as a ditzy cheerleader's attention span.

The bell rang.

"The drive-in's going to have another costume night," Matt added. "And people are already talking about acting out the movie."

"Maybe Alexander and I should get a cut of the admissions. Where's my agent when I need her?"

"Who was that creepy white-haired kid who came over to you by the movie screen?" Becky asked.

"I guess someone wanting to play one of the vampire gang," I replied, and slammed my locker shut. "But I thought he sucked," I added. "He wasn't convincing as an evil vampire at all."

20

Dancing in the Dark

There was a new girl in Dullsville—me. After all, I'd
spent sixteen years living a monotonous existence.
Now Dullsville wasn't so dull anymore. A few blocks away
from me on Benson Hill lived the love of my life—
Alexander Sterling. My boyfriend. My Gothic Mate. My
vampire.

I was reunited with Alexander, and his nemesis was
out of our lives. I had to wonder what would be normal
for us. I was dating a vampire. I would have to keep a
secret I'd never be able to share with Becky, my parents, or
anyone. To keep him in my life, I needed a padlock on my
black lips.

Alexander and I would always have to meet after
sundown. I would never be able to eat breakfast or lunch
with him. We'd have to avoid sitting near mirrors at
fancy restaurants and make sure garlic wasn't being

minced anywhere in the vicinity.

And most important, I wondered whether I would have to become a vampire for us to have a future.

That evening, I met Alexander at the Mansion door, a backpack slung on his shoulder and an umbrella in his hand.

"Let's go," he said proudly, taking my hand.

"Where are you taking me tonight? A tomb?"

"You'll see . . ."

"You were awesome that night. Everyone at school thought you totally rocked! For a moment, I thought you were really going to bite me."

"For a moment, I really wanted to," he said with a wink.

"It must be hard for you, resisting your impulses."

"You have impulses, too, that you resist, don't you?" he asked playfully, tickling me. "Why should I be any different?"

I giggled.

After a few blocks we stopped in front of Dullsville's country club.

"You're kidding. My dad belongs here."

"Well, he has good taste."

"I never thought so."

Bushes standing eight feet high lined the property of the golf course, surrounded by a low chain-link fence.

We quickly climbed over the metal blockade and walked onto Dullsville's golf course. Of all the places I've snuck into before, this was not on my list.

"If I get caught sneaking in here," I joked, "this could really ruin my reputation."

At night, the course seemed mysteriously spooky and gorgeous.

We walked across the tee, down the fairway, and onto the green, avoiding the sand traps and bunkers just like golf balls.

Alexander and I sat on the green of the third hole, which overlooked a small lake with a lit fountain. A few weeping willows, which offset the lake, in the darkness looked like they were crying black lace instead of leaves. The course was eerily quiet. The only sounds we could hear were crickets and the gentle splashing of the waterfall.

"I like to be surrounded by beautiful scenery—but you overshadow even that."

I gave him a quick kiss.

"I also like to dance in unusual places." He opened his backpack and pulled out a portable CD player. He switched it on, and Marilyn Manson began to wail.

"Can I have this dance?" he asked, offering his hand.

At first we slow danced on the green to one of the morbidly sluggish tunes. We must have looked like quite a sight—two goths dancing in the dark on a golf course.

As the songs picked up pace, we danced around each other and the flagpole until we were exhausted.

We ran to the lake and cupped our hands in the water. The light from the fountain caught my reflection in the water. What should have been Alexander's reflection was only ripples of water from where he dipped his hands. I looked up at him. He smiled back joyfully, not even aware of his missing image. I felt a pang of loneliness for him, wondering what it must be like to live a life of empty reflections.

Breathless, we plopped down on the green and looked up at the stars. The sky was clear except for some clouds in the distance. Lying on the open golf course without hovering trees and glaring streetlights, we could see what seemed like a million stars twinkling just for us.

Alexander sat up and pulled out two drinks from his backpack.

"Gummi worms, spiders, or lizards?" he asked, reaching back inside.

"Worms, please."

We both drank and chewed on the brightly colored candy insects.

"What's it like never seeing your reflection?" I asked, his missing image still on my mind.

"It's all I've ever known."

"How do you know what you look like?"

"From paintings. When I was five, my parents commissioned one of their artists to make a portrait of us. We have it hanging over the fireplace in our home in Romania. It was the most beautiful thing I'd ever seen. How the artist captured the light, the details of my mother's dimples, the joy in my father's eyes, all through gentle strokes from his palette. The artist made me look alive when I felt lonely and grim inside. That's the way this man saw me. I decided then that that's what I wanted to do."

"Did you like the way you looked?"

"I'm sure I looked much better than if I'd seen myself in a reflection." Alexander's voice became impassioned, as if he were expressing his thoughts for the very first time. "I always felt sorry for humans, spending so much time in front of the mirror. Fixing their hair, makeup, and clothes, mostly to impress others. Did they really see themselves in the mirror? Was it what they wanted to see? Did it make them feel good or bad? And mostly I wondered if they based their self-image on their reflected one."

"You're right. We do spend a lot of time worrying about our looks, instead of focusing on what's inside."

"The artist has the power to capture that. To express what he thinks about the subject. I thought that was much more romantic than seeing myself in a cold, stark glass reflection."

"So that is why you paint portraits? Like the one of me at the Snow Ball?"

"Yes."

"It must be hard to be an artist among vampires."

"That's why I never fit in. I'd rather create than destroy."

Alexander suddenly looked up at the moon. He got up and grabbed a sturdy branch that had fallen from one of the trees and was lying by the lake. He took off his belt and bound the branch to the umbrella handle. He removed the flagpole and stuck the umbrella stick in the third hole.

"What are you doing? Want to keep out the moon?"

Suddenly I could hear the sound of a sprinkler turning on. Water began to drizzle down over us like a gentle storm.

I giggled as the cold water hit my legs.

"This is so awesome! I never knew a golf course could be so beautiful."

We kissed underneath the sprinkling water until we noticed lightning flashing in the distance.

I quickly packed up our drinks and CD player while Alexander dismantled the umbrella.

"I'm sorry we have to call this short," he said as we headed for home.

"Are you kidding? It was perfect," I said, giving him a quick hug. "I'll never look at golf the same way again."

21

Creepy Carnival

For the next few days, I went to school, hung out with Becky and Matt, dodged Trevor, came home, and took care of Nightmare. After sunset, I spent as much time as I could with Alexander, watching movies, cuddling, and listening to music in the darkness.

By Saturday, I was exhausted. I slept the day away and met Alexander by dusk at his Mansion. It was the night of Dullsville's Spring Carnival.

In the past, Becky and I had always attended the carnival together. This time, we would be arriving separately on the arms of our respective dates.

Alexander and I entered, hand in hand, shortly after sunset. We stepped through the two arches made of multicolored balloons, a white wooden admission booth in between. Alexander approached Old Jim, who was selling tickets; Luke, his Great Dane, was sitting at his feet.

"Two, please," Alexander requested, paying for us both.

"I see you've been sleeping in one of the vacant coffins," Old Jim warned.

"I haven't slept at the cemetery for months," I replied. "Maybe it's—"

He looked at me skeptically. "Well, if I catch you, I have to tell your parents, you know."

Alexander grabbed my hand and led me away from Old Jim and through the balloon-filled entrance. The carnival was spread over Dullsville High's soccer field. There were booths of homemade pies, corn dogs, snow cones, rides like the Ferris wheel and the Scrambler, a fun house, and games of tic-tac-toe, a ring toss, and a dunking booth. The air smelled of cotton candy and grilled corn on the cob. Alexander and I walked through the crowd like the prince and princess of darkness. But he was oblivious to the stares and looked like a wide-eyed kid not knowing what to play with first.

"Haven't you been to a carnival before?" I asked.

"No. Have you?"

"Of course."

"You made it," I heard a familiar voice say. It was my dad.

I turned around to find my parents eating hot dogs at a picnic table.

Alexander shook my dad's hand and politely said hello to my mother.

"Would you like to sit with us?" my mom offered.

"They don't want to spend all day with us old fogies," my dad interjected. "You guys have fun," he said, reaching into his wallet and offering me a twenty.

"I've got it covered, Mr. Madison," Alexander said.

"I like your style," my dad replied, returning the money to his wallet.

"Thanks anyway, Dad," I said. "We'll see you later."

As Alexander and I walked past the booths, patrons and workers stared at us like we were part of the sideshow.

"Hey, Raven," Becky said, when I found her selling homemade pies at her father's booth. "Dad had to run home. We sold out of the caramel apples and only have two pies left."

"Congratulations," I complimented her. "But I was looking forward to some."

"I'll reserve two for you when he gets back," Matt said, as he handed a piece of apple cobbler to a customer.

"I think you've found your calling," I said to him.

We said good-bye to Becky and Matt as they tried to keep one step ahead of their customers.

On our way to the carnival rides, I spotted Ruby, who was standing in between two booths. "Hi, Ruby, are you here with Janice?" I asked.

"Oh, hi, Raven," she said, giving me a friendly hug. "No, I'm here with a friend," she added with a wink.

Just then Jameson, minus his usual butler uniform and wearing a dark suit and black tie, walked over with a fresh swirl of blue cotton candy.

"Hello, Miss Raven," he said, gently handing the candy to Ruby. "I'm glad to see Alexander is in such good hands, as I have the night off."

Alexander gave the Creepy Man a smile.

"I'm glad that you and Jameson are back in town," Ruby said to Alexander.

"I am, too," he replied, and squeezed my hand. "Is Jameson treating you right? I know he can get kind of wild," he teased.

"He's been nothing but a perfect gentleman," she said, but then whispered, "Hopefully that will wear off as the evening continues."

Alexander and I laughed. "We'll leave you two kids with your candy. I promised Raven I'd take her on the Ferris wheel."

We cut away from the food booths and past the carnival games.

"Raven," Billy Boy called from behind.

We turned around, and my brother ran up to us, holding a plastic bag with a frantic fish inside. Henry followed close behind with his own swimming prize.

"Look what we just won!" Billy Boy exclaimed.

"Cool," Alexander commented.

"He's a cutie," I said, tapping the side of the bag. "Just make sure you keep him out of reach of Nightmare. She's small now, but she'll be growing."

"Not to fear, I'm going to make a safety roof for their fishbowls," Henry proudly proclaimed.

"I'm sure you will," I said to my brother's nerd-mate.

"We're all out of tickets," Billy Boy whined. "Did you see Dad around?"

"Here," Alexander said, reaching in his back pocket

before I could answer. He handed Billy Boy some cash.

My brother's eyes bugged out as if he'd just won the lottery.

"Thanks, Alexander!" he exclaimed.

"Yeah, thanks, man," Henry said, and they took off back to the goldfish booth.

"That was so nice of you. You didn't have to do that," I said.

"Don't worry about it. Now let's go ride the Ferris wheel," he suggested.

Normally I hated waiting for rides and would cut in line, dragging along a reluctant Becky. Now I enjoyed the wait, because it meant I had more time with Alexander.

Soon we were ascending into the night sky. We slowly came to the top when the ride stopped, letting off the riders at the bottom.

"Do you think it will be difficult because we are different?" I asked, staring down at the couples.

"We are more alike than most."

"Does it bother you that we are not the same on the inside?" I asked, looking at him.

"But we are in here," he said, pointing to his heart.

"If I were Luna, would you have left the ceremony?"

Alexander looked confused. "What do you mean?"

"Do you want me to become a . . . ?" I asked.

Suddenly the ride started up, cutting our conversation short. We cuddled as our car finally descended to the ground.

Alexander helped me off the Ferris wheel. We paused,

overwhelmed by the choices of food, games, and rides that still awaited us.

"Let's do the ring toss," he said when we got off.

Alexander and I went over to the ring toss booth as a couple finished, walking away empty-handed.

I gazed at the stuffed animals as the blue-and-white-uniformed clerk, wearing a black top hat, picked up the rings off the floor.

"They're rigged. I never win. I usually spend all my allowance and I don't even get Mardi Gras beads," I lamented.

Alexander placed some money on the counter, and the clerk stood up and handed him three rings.

"Harder than it looks," I said.

Alexander stared at the single wooden pole as if he were a wolf staring at an unsuspecting deer.

He threw the rings in quick succession like a dealer at a casino. The clerk and I were stunned. The three rings were resting around the pole.

I jumped up and down. "You did it!"

Alexander beamed as the clerk handed me a giant purple bear. I squeezed it hard and gave Alexander a huge kiss.

I glowed as I held the bear, almost bigger than me.

"Snow cones are on me," I announced, as we turned to make our way back through the crowd. My stride was broken when I bumped into someone.

"Excuse me," I said, and placed the bear on my hip so I could see.

"Hey, monster, watch out!" Trevor hollered, holding two tickets. "On your way to get your face painted?" he asked. "Perhaps you should."

"Nice seeing you, too," I said sarcastically.

I grabbed Alexander's hand, and we headed toward the snow cones.

"Hey, Luna!" I heard Trevor call from behind.

Alexander and I stopped dead in our tracks. He couldn't have just said what we thought he said.

"Luna!" Trevor called again.

Alexander and I looked at each other in disbelief.

Luna? It couldn't be! Jagger's twin sister? What would she be doing in Dullsville?

We turned around to find Trevor looking toward the fun house—a huge multicolored rectangular building. On the upper left-hand side of the structure was a gigantic clown's head, his mouth the entrance to the exhibit. On the bottom right-hand side, patrons exited through the red fabric laces of the clown's enormous brown shoe.

"That *is* her," Alexander said, shakily pointing to a petite girl standing near the front of the ramp that led to the entrance. She had long, flowing powder white hair and pale porcelain white skin, and she was wearing a pastel pink dress and black boots.

"It's like seeing an apparition. The last time I saw her was in Romania."

"What is she doing here?" I asked. "It's not like this town is vacation central."

"That's what I want to know!"

I handed the bear to Alexander, and we hurried after her, catching up to Trevor.

"You know that girl?" I asked Trevor, my pulse racing.

"A friend of Alexander's introduced us and asked me to bring her here. She's really pretty," he said in my face. "Why, are you jealous?"

"Jagger? He's still here?" I asked, confused.

"If you really were a good friend of his, you'd know that."

"He's not a friend. He's evil. You can't trust him," I warned.

"Well, he is kind of freaky like you guys, but he said he'd had a falling out with Alexander, so I figured that made him cool."

"He talked to you more than that night outside the Mansion?"

"What, are you spying on me? He came to a night game and told me his sister was coming to town. He asked me if I'd want to meet her. The coach wouldn't let him on the field, though. That dude has more metal on his face than a pair of cleats."

"Jagger's not a replacement for Matt, you know," I tried to tell Trevor. "He's nothing like Matt. Jagger's just trying to play you."

"Sounds like someone is jealous."

"He's not what you think he is," Alexander urgently cautioned.

"Listen, it was wonderful talking to you, but I have a date. Besides, you better get back to your cage. I think the

161

zoo has reported you missing."

He took off into the crowd. We began to follow but were stopped when a burly man holding a toddler stepped in our way. I could see Trevor and Luna racing up the red, tongued ramp of the fun house.

"The end of the line is back there!" the burly man ordered, pointing behind us.

"It's urgent," I said.

I peered past the disgruntled fun house customer and saw Trevor handing his tickets to the clerk. They stepped into the clown's mouth and disappeared.

I grabbed Alexander's hand, and we raced around the man as he wiped ice cream off his child's mouth.

We hurried up the plank and around the patrons in line. "Hey, no cutting!" a few kids started shouting.

When we reached the entrance, the clerk blocked our way. "Tickets, please."

"I don't . . ." I reached into my pocket and pulled out a handful of change and put it into his palm.

"That's only enough for one."

Alexander pulled out a wad of dollars, stuck it into the clerk's hand, and placed the bear at his feet. "I'll be back for him," Alexander said. He grabbed my hand, and we raced through the clown's mouth.

We stepped into a room filled with multicolored plastic balls up to our knees. We waded through the balls, trying to move as quickly as possible.

"At this rate, we'll never find her," I said.

When we finally reached the end of the room, we saw

that to the right of us was a red door, to the left a black-and-white tunnel.

"Oh no! It's a maze!" I groaned. "Should we flip a coin?"

"We don't have time," Alexander said.

I followed him through a huge black-and-white tunnel that twisted around us as we walked. I got dizzy, stumbling, holding on to the railing and Alexander for support. We had to walk over a glass bridge. I could see Trevor below. I banged on the glass, but he didn't look up.

At the end of the bridge, there was a red slide. I went down first, with Alexander following behind. When we rose to our feet, I saw Trevor's blond hair ten feet ahead of me.

"Trevor—" I called.

But he turned the corner, heading into the next room. I pushed past a family of three and opened a polka dotted door.

Alexander and I were alone.

"Trevor?" I called.

The lights went out. I stood frozen. We could hear the maniacal laughter of a clown as soft lights slowly dimmed. And then Luna appeared before us.

She was beautiful. Ocean blue eyes, puffy pink lips, brilliant baby-doll black eyelashes. Her pale bubblegum-colored cotton dress outlined in fuchsia lace hung on her. Her skinny alabaster white legs poked out of her chunky black knee-high boots, a plastic pink Scare Bear dangling from the zipper. On her upper arm was a tattoo of a black rose.

Before we could speak, it went totally dark.

Alexander grabbed my hand just as the room slowly began to brighten, the black walls now glass. Luna was still standing before us.

I caught my reflection. The wall wasn't glass after all, but a hall of mirrors.

Dozens of Ravens reflected on and on. Alexander, still standing beside me, didn't reflect back. There was one other reflection that was missing.

I was breathless.

"What have you come for?" Alexander challenged her.

"Luna!" I could hear Trevor call from another room. "Where are you?"

Luna smiled a wicked pale smile, two sparkling fangs glistening. I gasped.

"Well, if you've gotten your wish—to become a vampire," Alexander said, "then why are you here?"

"Jagger sent for me. Now I want to live the life I was never able to before. Jagger gave me an opportunity to get out of Romania."

"What about the vampire who bit you? Shouldn't you be with him?" Alexander argued.

"He was just a fling, on unsacred ground. After you left me, I realized I could find someone else—anyone else—to transform me and find true love later."

"You can find that in Romania," Alexander disputed.

"*You* didn't," she said with an evil glare. "Besides, Jagger told me he met a guy who he thought might be perfect for me."

"Trevor?" I asked. "You've got to be kidding."

"But you can't trust Jagger," Alexander argued. "He's not looking out for your best interest, only his own. He's motivated by revenge."

"Now that I'm in your world, I see things differently. I saw it in your eyes at the cemetery, Alexander. We both want the same thing," she said. "Vampire or human. I just want a relationship I can sink my teeth into."

The lights went out. I squeezed Alexander's hand tightly. I reached out blindly. I had to find Trevor before Luna did.

"Trevor!" I called. "Don't—"

The light flashed on again.

Luna was gone.

Acknowledgments

I am forever grateful to my editor, Katherine Tegen, for your extreme talent, friendship, direction, and enthusiasm. A sequel would not have been possible without you.

To my agent, Ellen Levine, I am extremely thankful for your advice, expertise, and friendship.

Many thanks to Julie Hittman, for all your hard work, helpful e-mails, and upbeat nature.

And hugs to my brother, Mark Schreiber, for your continuing generosity and support.